'Ooh, sorry!'

Nicky realised that she w□□ □ing across Jason's chest. The fasten□□□ □□ □at had worked loose and she w□□ □□□ □□□ □are skin.

She began to ex□□ □□□ □□ her embarrassing po□□ □□□ □s hands on her shoulde□

'Why be sor□□ □□□ □'s rather nice to be snuggling u□ □□ □□ □-haired beauty in the middle of a cr□□ □□ □nis.'

To her shock and surprise, his voice was husky, decidedly sexy as he looked down at her. His eyes were warm, tender almost, and she caught a glimpse of the intense interest he'd shown in her on that first evening. Thinking of the brutal, heartless way he'd treated her flatmate, Nicky felt an uncontrollable anger welling up inside her.

But in that moment she had a blinding flash of inspiration. Maybe she could teach him a lesson in commitment he wouldn't forget in a hurry!

As a full-time writer, mother and grandmother, **Margaret Barker** says: 'I feel blessed with my lifestyle, which has evolved over the years and included working as a State Registered Nurse. My husband and I live in a sixteenth-century thatched house near the East Anglian Coast. We are still very much in love, which helps when I am describing the romantic feelings of my heroines. In fact, if I find the creative flow diminishing, my husband will often suggest we put in some more research into the romantic aspects that are eluding me at the time!'

Recent titles by the same author:

THE PREGNANT DOCTOR
RELUCTANT PARTNERS

A CHRISTMAS TO REMEMBER

BY
MARGARET BARKER

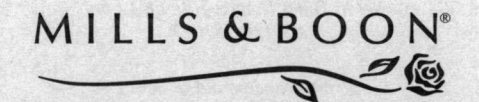

MILLS & BOON

DID YOU PURCHASE THIS BOOK WITHOUT A COVER?

If you did, you should be aware it is **stolen property** as it was reported *unsold and destroyed* by a retailer. Neither the author nor the publisher has received any payment for this book.

All the characters in this book have no existence outside the imagination of the author, and have no relation whatsoever to anyone bearing the same name or names. They are not even distantly inspired by any individual known or unknown to the author, and all the incidents are pure invention.

All Rights Reserved including the right of reproduction in whole or in part in any form. This edition is published by arrangement with Harlequin Enterprises II B.V. The text of this publication or any part thereof may not be reproduced or transmitted in any form or by any means, electronic or mechanical, including photocopying, recording, storage in an information retrieval system, or otherwise, without the written permission of the publisher.

This book is sold subject to the condition that it shall not, by way of trade or otherwise, be lent, resold, hired out or otherwise circulated without the prior consent of the publisher in any form of binding or cover other than that in which it is published and without a similar condition including this condition being imposed on the subsequent purchaser.

MILLS & BOON and MILLS & BOON with the Rose Device are registered trademarks of the publisher.

*First published in Great Britain 2001
Harlequin Mills & Boon Limited,
Eton House, 18-24 Paradise Road, Richmond, Surrey TW9 1SR*

© Margaret Barker 2001

ISBN 0 263 82707 0

*Set in Times Roman 10½ on 12 pt.
03-1201-51017*

*Printed and bound in Spain
by Litografia Rosés, S.A., Barcelona*

CHAPTER ONE

THE wretched man had taken the last parking space! Nicky had been aware of this black sports car behind her all the way up the hill from Highdale village and for some reason it had made her nervous. It was pouring with rain and when it rained in the Yorkshire Dales it could turn into a real deluge, like today!

She'd been driving slowly, unsure of the way to Greystones, Patricia's and Adam's house, when up came this sleek, streamlined car behind her at a frightening pace. It was true that the driver had had the decency to slow down and keep some way behind her, but all the same she'd felt intimidated and desperately aware that she was holding him up. In her rear-view mirror, in spite of the poor visibility she'd been able to make out the fact that the driver was male, probably of the type who would be tapping his fingers impatiently on his expensive walnut dashboard.

Following the printed instructions that Patricia had given her, Nicky had hoped to shake him off as she turned down the little lane that led to the house she was looking for, but annoyingly he turned off as well. What was worse, he slowed down as she drove through the balloon-festooned gates and followed her up the drive to the house. There were masses of cars parked in front of the house and she'd cruised carefully along one side of the parking area, looking for a space. Meanwhile, old smarty pants, whoever he was, had gone swiftly around the other side and nipped smartly into the last space.

She could have parked on the grass, but even in this

rainstorm she could see that the lawn was well manicured and wouldn't look good with deep muddy tyre marks. Nicky glanced down despondently at the papers on her lap, the instructions of how to get here and the invitation to two-year-old Emma's birthday party. She hadn't wanted to come in the first place but, being the new doctor at Highdale Practice, she couldn't very well cry off this opportunity to meet some of her colleagues and their various children.

Maybe she could just turn round and go back the way she'd come, pretend she'd got lost in the storm or the car had broken down. Parking on the grass was out of the question if she wanted to keep on the right side of her fellow doctors. Nicky reached into the glove compartment for some tissues and wiped the windscreen which was already steaming up. It was absolutely pelting with rain now and, even assuming she could find somewhere to ditch the car, she would get soaking wet walking across to the house.

The tapping sound on her side window made her jump. Looking up, she saw the ghostly outline of a man. She wound down the window. The apparition was clutching an umbrella and as he stooped to speak to her, shrouded completely in waterproofs, he looked like someone who'd survived a shipwreck.

'You seem to be stuck here. There's a sign on the other side saying there's more parking round the back of the house, but you won't have been able to see it in all this rain. I noticed you were having problems so I've just moved my car from over there. You can have the space I was in.'

The rain was spattering in on Nicky's new suit. 'Thanks. I'd better close the window.'

'Have you got an umbrella?' he asked in a deep, gravelly voice.

The voice intrigued her. Where had she heard it before? There was something very familiar about this stranger but she couldn't made out his features in the shadow cast by the umbrella and the hood of the anorak he'd pulled down over his face to keep out the rain.

'No, I haven't brought an umbrella but the house is only over there so...'

Her voice trailed away. The house was a good way from the parking spaces and she would get soaking wet. She thought she detected a smile under the hood. There was a flash of white teeth and then he spoke again in that intriguingly familiar voice. They had met before—she was sure of it now—but where?

'Tell you what, I'll jump in beside you,' he said firmly, 'and then I can escort you to the house under the umbrella.'

There was a flash of lightning followed very quickly by a loud clap of thunder.

'Thanks.' Nicky wound up the window. As she leaned across to open the passenger door she realised this was obviously the man she'd found so intimidating as he'd followed her up the hill. When he'd driven into that last parking space she'd never imagined he would turn out to be so helpful.

He pushed back the hood before shrugging off the anorak he'd been wearing round his shoulders as he settled into the passenger seat beside her. She took a long, hard look at him and had to suppress the gasp that threatened to escape her lips. She could see the expression of astonishment on his face as he turned to look at her.

'We've met before, haven't we?' he said slowly, his voice quiet now. 'You're Sue's flatmate, aren't you?'

She looked into those emerald, slightly mocking eyes and had to prevent herself from giving a shiver of horror.

Jason Carmichael, the man who'd had such a ruinous impact on poor Sue's life.

'*Was* Sue's flatmate. We met at Sue's dinner party,' she said, in a toneless voice, as the memories tumbled back.

Looking at him now, she remembered how she'd been drawn towards this undeniably handsome, seemingly charming man. He'd sat opposite her and they'd had so much to talk about that she'd become oblivious to the buzz of conversation going on around her. They'd discovered they were both doctors but had avoided discussing their medical work while they'd concentrated on the non-professional side of their lives.

She'd loved the way his longish brown hair had fallen down over his forehead whenever he'd laughed or moved his head. And that voice! She'd thought she would have loved to have listened to those gravelly, sexy tones for a long time to come.

When they'd got to the coffee stage and had moved into the sitting area, Sue, who'd drunk rather a lot of wine, had asked Nicky to take over as hostess so she could go to bed and sleep it off. At the end of the evening when the guests had been leaving, Jason had held back until just the two of them had remained. He'd said he would help her to clear up, but it had soon become apparent that neither of them had wanted to waste time in the kitchen.

They'd gone back into the living room. Nicky had kicked off her shoes and curled up on the sofa next to Jason. The next thing she'd remembered had been his arm around her shoulders, the closeness of his virile body as she'd turned towards him. And then the feel of his lips on hers had begun to drive her wild with anticipation. She'd managed to hold onto her senses just long enough to stem the inevitable love-making, even though she remembered that, uncharacteristically for her on a first encounter, she'd been desperately tempted to go the whole way.

She pulled herself away before they'd reached the point of no return, sat up and ran her hands through her dishevelled hair. Jason whispered that they must meet again soon. The feeling was mutual. At the time she thought that she couldn't wait the couple of days to the dinner date Jason had proposed.

His kiss was infinitely tender as he left the flat. But as she closed the door, she found Sue standing across the room, her face as black as thunder. Nicky's flatmate explained in no uncertain terms that Jason was hers. She'd been seeing him for years and lately their romance had taken off to the point that she was expecting him to propose soon.

Nicky's first reaction was to think what a swine he was to have taken advantage of the fact that Sue was incapacitated so that he could two-time her. Granted, she'd been a willing partner but she'd had no idea that Jason and Sue were an item. She felt that if he could behave in such a cavalier manner towards Sue, she'd give him a taste of his own medicine. So she didn't even bother to cancel the date. She simply didn't turn up.

She avoided taking his phone calls by simply giving the receiver to Sue whenever she heard his voice at the other and then leaving the room so that she wouldn't get involved. If Sue wasn't in, she simply hung up on him.

And when, a few months later, his behaviour towards Sue was completely unforgivable, she realised that he really was the lowest of the low and she'd had a lucky escape.

'Jason Carmichael,' he said now, 'in case you've forgotten my name.'

'I remember,' Nicky told him, switching on the engine

and looking in the rear-view mirror. How could she have forgotten? 'Damn! Someone's just taken that space.'

'Reverse over there and you'll see a gap in the trees that leads to the back of the house, Nicky.'

She bridled as he used her name as if they were old friends, instead of dire enemies. 'So you haven't forgotten my name.'

'Well, we did talk a lot to each other that night.'

What an understatement!

'But I don't think you told me your surname.'

She crashed the gears as she began to reverse. Her hands were shaking from the impact of meeting up again with this two-faced man.

'Nicky Devlin.'

'Small world! What are you doing up here in Yorkshire?'

'I'm about to start work at Highdale Practice.'

There was a long pause before he spoke again. 'So am I,' he said quietly.

Nicky ground the car to a halt beneath a tree. Water was pouring down off the leaves like a waterfall, cascading over her windscreen.

She drew in her breath at the startling news. 'I didn't know they'd appointed two new doctors.'

'Neither did I,' Jason said, in a neutral tone.

She put her hand on the door, feeling she wanted to get away from the claustrophobic atmosphere of the car. 'We'd better go in.'

'I'll come round and hold the umbrella over you.'

'Don't worry. I can make a dash for it.'

The last thing she wanted was to be jammed under an umbrella in close proximity to a man like Jason Carmichael. How on earth she was going to work with him she didn't know—she would have to cross that bridge when she came to it.

Her long auburn hair was soaked by the time she reached the back door of the house. Nicky stood in the porch, shaking herself like a dog who'd just been swimming. Jason Carmichael was behind her, closing his umbrella and depositing it in a stand beside the door.

The door opened and Patricia Drayton, one of the doctors who'd been on the interview panel, smiled in welcome.

'Nicky! You found us. I was beginning to think you'd taken a wrong turning. It's not an easy location to find. I'm so glad you're here.'

Nicky found Patricia's effusive welcome comforting. It helped to calm her after the shock of meeting up with Jason Carmichael again.

'And Jason, too! I hadn't seen you standing in the shadows there. Come on in, both of you. Have you been introduced?'

'We met in London some time ago,' Jason said, handing over a large beribboned parcel to his hostess. 'This is for Emma and these are for you, Patricia.'

Nicky could discern the effect that Jason's wide, dazzling smile had on Patricia, the happily married mother. She wondered if he had this effect on all the women he spoke to. She couldn't help remembering how she'd been completely bowled over when he'd smiled at her across the table.

He was handing a bouquet of flowers to Patricia who looked utterly charmed by him. At her interview, she'd noticed the wonderful rapport between Patricia and her husband, Dr Adam Young. They were the perfect example of a couple in love. But even in her married bliss, when a personable charmer like Jason Carmichael came along, it was obvious that Patricia hadn't forgotten how to appreciate the opposite sex from a detached, aesthetic point of view.

The phrase that sprang to Nicky's mind was that he could have charmed the birds from the trees! And she knew from bitter experience that he would use that charm to ruthless advantage when he needed to. She pulled the picture book she'd bought for Emma from her shoulder bag. The coloured wrapping paper tore as she extricated it past the zip.

'At least it's dry,' she said as she held the parcel out towards Patricia. 'This is for Emma.'

Patricia smiled. 'You're both so kind. Perhaps you'd like to give your presents to the birthday girl. She loves unwrapping things.'

The huge farmhouse-type kitchen was crowded. Children scampered everywhere, babies were hugged by caring mothers, anxious their little ones shouldn't be trampled in the crush. But in spite of the chaotic atmosphere, Nicky began to feel that she was glad she'd come. It would certainly break the ice with the colleagues she would have to work with. Some of them had brought their little ones with them.

Patricia ushered her over to meet her daughter. Two-year-old Emma was a pretty, dark-haired child and Nicky warmed immediately towards her as the little girl put on a winning smile.

'This is Nicky,' Patricia told her daughter.

'Hello, Nicky. Ooh, thank you for the present.'

Chubby arms were held out in excited anticipation at the sight of the wrapped parcel and tiny hands were soon tearing at the paper.

'It's a picture book, Mummy. Ooh, look at this little cat…and this mouse…'

Emma's eyes were deflected from the book as another, larger present appeared. Jason's expensive doll soon captured all her attention.

'Our new colleagues are here, everybody,' Patricia called

out above the noise of the squeals and chattering. 'Nicky and Jason, valuable members of staff come to rescue us all from overwork.'

There were cries of welcome from the adults and Nicky felt again that she was going to enjoy working at Highdale Practice.

'Come and meet my other children.' Patricia whisked Nicky away from the crowd around the birthday girl and, pressing through the crush, moved to the other side of the enormous kitchen.

'Rebecca is Adam's daughter by his first marriage,' she said quietly as they approached a pretty little girl who was blowing up balloons for a couple of younger boys who were noisily appropriating as many as they could and popping a few in the process.

'Rebecca, this is Nicky who's going to do some of my work now that I'm only going to work two days a week.'

Rebecca smiled up at her. 'Hi, Nicky. Would you like a balloon? Stop it, Theo! Rowan, put that balloon down! Wait your turn. This one's for Nicky, because she's new here and she needs a present.'

Nicky thanked Rebecca as she accepted her balloon. 'And how old are you, Rebecca?'

'Six and a quarter,' the little girl said proudly. 'These are my brothers, Theo and Rowan, and they're only three. That's why they behave so badly. My mummy says that when they're as old as me they'll know how to be good but I'm not sure about that.'

Patricia was moving her on again, this time into an oak-panelled hall that led to a curving staircase. 'Come up and see our baby. Little Matthew is four months and he sleeps in the afternoon.'

Nicky deposited her balloon on the antique table near the

front door. 'I'll take that home as a memento of Emma's party.'

Patricia turned and smiled. 'Emma will be so pleased you like it.'

They were climbing the staircase. Nicky paused, looking around her admiringly as they reached the landing. 'It's a beautiful house, Patricia.'

'Thank you. It was Adam's house before we got married last Christmas. It's turned out to be a super family house. Adam's daughter Rebecca begged to be able to live with us, and my own daughter, Emma, from a previous relationship had already claimed Adam as her favourite daddy. Then came the icing on the cake when we had our own baby, Matthew. It's a case of yours, mine and ours.'

Nicky was intrigued. 'And the boys who were waiting for the balloons that Rebecca was blowing up? Where do they fit in?'

'Theo and Rowan are the twin sons of Adam's ex-wife Lauren, who is, of course, Rebecca's mother, and her husband Tony. The twins spend a lot of time here because Lauren has just had a new baby and is finding it difficult to cope.'

Patricia broke off and smiled. 'Actually, although Lauren loves her children, she's not really the maternal type so I'm doing everything I can to ease the load on her. I know Rebecca prefers her mummy to be in a good mood when she sees her. Adam and I were delighted when Lauren announced that she and Tony were going to have another baby. Only a year ago they were contemplating divorce. Then Tony had a heart attack and made a great effort to change his excessive lifestyle and they got back together again. But Lauren finds looking after the new baby and the twins difficult.'

Nicky smiled down at her diminutive colleague. Who would have thought that this tiny, fragile-looking blonde was a doctor and a busy mum?

'You obviously love children. So, let me get this straight. It's just Rebecca, Emma and Matthew who live here, isn't it?'

'And Adam and me,' Patricia said softly.

It was something about the way Patricia spoke her husband's name that tore at Nicky's heartstrings. She'd never thought that love could be visible but in this case it was positively palpable.

'I think I detect an ongoing romance here,' she said gently.

Patricia sighed. 'It wasn't easy, getting to this stage. There were so many complications after we first met but, oh, it was worth it!'

'I can see that.' Nicky could feel a lump rising in her throat. For a brief moment she allowed herself the luxury of wondering what married love would be like if she ever got around to it.

She'd seen so many unhappy marriages that, at the ripe old age of twenty-nine, she sometimes wondered if she was in danger of turning into an old cynic! She wouldn't want to be part of that sort of situation, not when she could keep her own independent, interesting lifestyle. A man would have to be very special to make her change what she had now!

She followed Patricia to an open bedroom door and peeped inside. A small, blond-haired, sleeping baby remained blissfully unaware that he was being admired as Nicky and his mother stood either side of his cot.

'He's lovely!' Nicky breathed. The next second she

found herself thinking that it would be almost worth giving up her independence to have a baby like this.

But no, that definitely wasn't on the cards. She had an awful lot of living to do before she embarked on such a seriously important step. It was true that her biological clock was ticking away. Next year, when she was thirty, she knew she would have to resist any treacherous feelings of broodiness—unless she'd met Mr Right by then, which was highly unlikely.

She could hear someone coming along the landing. Both she and Patricia turned at the same moment. Jason Carmichael was standing in the doorway. She couldn't help thinking that he looked the part of Mr Right on the surface but, knowing all the treachery he was capable of, it made him a complete non-starter. In fact, out of a possible ten marks as a candidate for her baby's father, she would give him a minus five.

'Adam told me to come up and see baby Matthew,' he whispered.

Patricia smiled as he went over to her side of cot. 'What do you think?'

'I think he's wonderful!' came the reply.

Nicky turned away and moved towards the door. She couldn't bear the sight of that two-faced monster admiring someone else's baby after he'd insisted that Sue's pregnancy, which would have led to him being a father, should be terminated.

She was acutely aware that Patricia and Jason were following her down the stairs. Jason was actually saying how much he loved babies. Apparently, it transpired that he'd considered specialising in obstetrics but had gone into general practice instead.

'May you be forgiven,' she whispered under her breath

as she grabbed hold of the polished rail at the bottom of the stairs to steady herself.

'Are you all right, Nicky?' Patricia asked gently.

Nicky swallowed hard. 'I'm fine! Nearly missed my step, that's all.'

'You need some refreshment. Come into the kitchen. Adam should be dispensing the champagne by now.'

She readily accepted the proffered glass from Patricia's handsome husband. One glass of champagne wouldn't affect her drive home in a couple of hours if she ate some sandwiches and drank a couple of glasses of water. She needed something to dispel the feeling of gloom at the prospect of having to work with that master of duplicity!

Looking around her, Nicky saw that the adults had gravitated to one end of the kitchen where a makeshift bar had been set up on a long wooden table. The children were now gathered around the kitchen, tucking into crisps, sausages and little sandwiches. Jason, she noticed, was in deep conversation with a very attractive young woman she recognised as Barbara, one of the part-time nurses from the practice. Typical! His face was animated as he talked. She found herself hoping he wasn't telling Barbara how he loved babies.

'Hi, Nicky! How're you settling in?'

Jane, the senior partner at Highdale Practice, was standing in front of her. Nicky noticed that Jane's pregnancy was decidedly more advanced now than when she'd attended her interview. She tried to remember when the baby was due—New Year perhaps? She remembered someone telling her that Jane was the third generation in the practice and responsible for the expansion programme that had been necessary when the new housing estate and the holiday village had been built. On the interview panel Nicky had established an immediate rapport with Jane.

A tall, slim woman, she had a rather plain face but she was always pleasant and helpful and a kind of inner joy seemed to radiate from her. Jane was another lucky person in love with her husband apparently, and it showed.

'Fine, thanks! Well, moving house is never easy, even if you only have a few possessions. My bedsit in London was furnished but I still had to bring my computer and my CD player and all the clothes I'll probably never wear again but can't bear to throw away, plus the seemingly invaluable books and the clutter of several years of city living.'

Jane laughed. 'I count myself lucky I was born up at Highdale House which used to be my home and a surgery before we needed to expand. Even so, it took several journeys with a van to remove all my clutter when I went to live at Fellside with Richard.'

'Where is Richard this afternoon?' Nicky asked, casting her eyes around the crowded room.

Jane grinned. 'Someone's got to hold the fort. Poor Richard drew the short straw today. He's up at the practice with two of our part-time nurses, giving flu jabs to our senior citizens. The flu vaccination programme worked well last winter and we're not taking any chances this year either. We've had a massive advertising campaign to bring them all in before our famously severe Yorkshire winter sets in. The only thing is, we've been too successful and with the influx of more retired residents to the new housing estate we're overstretched in terms of doctor power. You wouldn't believe how happy we all are to have you and Jason aboard!'

'You've certainly all made me feel welcome,' Nicky said. 'Patricia let me have the small house she used to live in before she was married. Adam had bought it as an investment apparently, and they've been terribly kind about asking a very small rent. I couldn't believe how cheap it was after the London prices I've been paying for a crummy bedsit.'

She took a sip of her champagne. Jason, she noticed with alarm, was making his way over.

Jane smiled. 'Ah, Jason! I was just telling Nicky how glad we are to have some more medical colleagues. The fact is I gave up work last week. I'd virtually stopped anyway, but I was just tying up a few loose ends. I'm going to be housebound from next week until after the baby is born.' She pulled a face before adding, 'Doctor's orders!'

'What's the problem, Jane?' Jason asked quietly.

Nicky noticed the look of deep concern on Jason's face. Maybe he cared about what happened to other people's babies but not his own. She fervently hoped this was the case, otherwise he wouldn't make a very good doctor.

'My last scan revealed I've got placenta praevia.'

'I'm so sorry about that,' Jason said, his voice sympathetic. 'What kind, exactly?'

Jane pursed her lips. 'The worst possible scenario. My baby's placenta is completely covering the internal os so, as everybody knows, as the uterus continues to grow I may experience some bleeding. I sailed through my first pregnancy when I produced Edward a couple of years ago, but this time I'm not so lucky.'

'When is the baby due?' Nicky asked, trying to disguise her alarm.

She was reflecting that placenta praevia was a very serious condition. It occurred when the placenta was situated in the lower segment of the womb. As the womb stretched, there would inevitably be bleeding as the placenta became partially separated from it.

'Baby's not due until mid-January, but James Beecham, my consultant, doesn't want to take any chances.'

'Quite right!' Jason said. 'James Beecham, did you say? Not a tall man with bushy black eyebrows, balding on top, about my age?'

Jane was smiling. 'That's James. Perfect description! You obviously know him.'

'We were at medical school together in London. We'd both decided to specialise in obstetrics but I got called back to Norfolk to sort out a crisis in the family medical practice for my father. After a few years as a GP I decided to abandon my ambitions in obstetrics.'

'That must have been a terrible wrench for you,' Nicky said coldly. 'I mean, not being able to spend all day caring for pregnant women and delivering babies.'

His expression was enigmatic as he looked down at her. 'It was, actually. But I got over it when I discovered how fulfilling general practice could be.'

As Nicky turned away, she found she was trembling. Sooner or later she was going to have to have it out with Dr Two-Faced Carmichael. She couldn't allow this bitterness to simmer without any sort of explanation from him. Perhaps he would do the honourable thing and proffer an explanation as soon as they were alone together.

'Small world, isn't it?' Jane said, sipping her orange juice. 'Fancy you knowing James Beecham, Jason. And Patricia tells me you've met Nicky before.'

'Only once,' Nicky put in quickly. 'Jason came to a dinner party in London given by my flatmate, Sue.'

'Is Sue a doctor?' Jane asked.

'No, she's an actress...or rather was an actress before... She's with her parents in Australia at the moment.'

Nicky was intensely aware that Jason was watching her. She could feel her cheeks beginning to burn.

Jason leaned forward towards her. She could feel his warm breath on her face and thought she could detect some kind of aftershave which would have been distinctly provocative if she hadn't hated the man.

'I've kind of lost touch with her recently. Is she going to stay long with her parents?' Jason said.

'I've no idea.'

She couldn't bear the innocent expression on his face, the very man who'd caused poor Sue to go running back to her parents because she couldn't stand London with all its reminders of him. Nicky could feel herself boiling inside but she was trying desperately to remain calm.

'I can see you two have a lot of catching up to do so, if you'll excuse me...' Jane said as she moved away, leaving a reluctant Nicky alone with Jason. Luckily Adam joined them so she didn't have to say anything further about Sue.

The kitchen phone was ringing. Patricia eased her way through the crush and picked it up. 'You'll have to speak up... Yes, this is Dr Patricia...' She listened for a few moments before putting down the phone and crossing back to the adults' table.

'Adam, the emergency services just called me. There's been a car crash near the end of our drive. The ambulances are on their way but they've been held up by a tree blocking the road. Apparently, one of the car crash victims has gone into labour. They've asked if we could—'

'I'll go,' Jason said quickly. 'Adam and Patricia should stay here with their guests. Perhaps Nicky would come with me?'

She was aware of those emerald, slightly mocking eyes looking down at her as he threw out the challenge. Yes, challenge, that's what it would be. A testing time to see if she could put her hatred aside long enough to do a good professional job. Maybe they would be called upon to save lives, deliver a baby. Whatever it was, she was determined to do the best she could and put her animosity towards Jason out of her mind.

'Jason's right,' she said. 'Adam and Patricia must stay here and take care of their children. We'll deal with the emergency.'

CHAPTER TWO

NEITHER of them spoke as Jason's black sports car hurtled towards the gates. Nicky had put herself into a state of truce. They were both experienced doctors. That was all that mattered. They were a couple of professionals on a lifesaving mission.

As Jason turned the car out into the storm-torn lane, Nicky gasped in horror. In spite of all her years of training and working as a doctor, the sight of a traffic accident always affected her. There would be people inside the tangled wreckage of what looked like a head-on collision between a small blue car and a ramshackle lorry. A tall man, shrouded in an anorak, was leaning over the side of the car, shouting to the occupants inside.

The rain was still lashing relentlessly down whilst the wind whipped the autumn leaves into tornado spirals that only added more problems to the diminishing, late afternoon visibility. The headlights illuminated the disturbing scene as Jason pulled on the handbrake and leapt out of the car.

'Are you the doctor?' the distraught man said, attempting to wipe the rain from his face as he turned to face Jason.

'There's a woman in the back of this car about to have a baby, so she tells me, and it looks like she's right. They were on their way to the maternity ward at Moortown General when this lorry crashed into them. That's her husband but he's passed out, poor soul, like the driver of that lorry that bumped into them. We live just up the lane, so I got my wife to phone for the ambulance.'

'Go and check on the lorry driver, Nicky,' Jason said tersely. 'I'll help the woman in the back here.'

Nicky quickly went over to look inside the cab of the lorry. The lorry driver was swearing loudly about the pain in his leg, but it looked as if he would survive. Luckily his door was hanging open so she would be able to get to him. She extricated a syringe from the emergency bag that Patricia had given her and, carefully climbing up, she leant into the cab and clasped the man's hand.

'I'm Nicky Devlin. I'm a doctor. Would you like to tell me your name?'

'Harry Marshall. And this bloody leg hurts like hell.'

Nicky could see that Harry wasn't exaggerating. From the unnatural angle of the lower right leg, which had obviously been jammed against the handbrake, she deduced there was a possible fracture of one or both of the two bones. Either the tibia or the fibula could be broken. But after a quick examination, the rest of him seemed in relatively good shape and she decided he would be OK until the emergency services arrived to take over.

'I'm going to give you a shot of something to ease the pain,' she said, reaching into the pocket of the anorak Patricia had lent her. 'After that, I'm afraid you'll have to wait a bit longer until the emergency services get through, but I'll do what I can when I've seen to the other patients here. We've got a woman who's gone into labour in the car and her husband's in pretty bad shape.'

Nicky leaned further inside the cab, the syringe poised in her hand. 'Now, just relax, Harry, while I... That's fine.'

'That poor woman!' Harry said, in a sympathetic tone, completely forgetting his own predicament. 'I wouldn't wish that on anybody. Having a baby is bad enough at the best of times. I should know. Me and the missus have had six of the little blighters, one of them born on the bathroom floor, but at least I could make her comfortable afterwards. Will she be all right? I must have skidded on them wet leaves and the next I knew that little car was smack into me.'

'My colleague is doing what he can to help her,' Nicky said. 'I've got to check on her husband and then—'

'Don't you worry about me, Doctor. I'm not planning on going anywhere in this lousy weather, so I'll just sit here and keep still. But you won't forget me, will you?'

Nicky smiled and patted his hand. 'I'll be back as soon as I can, Harry.'

She climbed back down, tearing the cloth on one knee of her new trouser suit on a piece of jagged metal. What did it matter? A mere detail when measured against the enormity of the suffering of her patients. She found the driver of the blue car was still unconscious but breathing easily. There was a cut on his forehead where he'd obviously hit his head on the steering-wheel. The wound would need cleaning and stitching. She leaned inside and took his pulse. It was faint but steady. Very shortly, she hoped, he would come round if it was concussion and nothing more serious. There didn't seem to be any more apparent injuries.

Nicky turned her attention to the pregnant woman on the back seat. Jason, with the help of the local man, had somehow managed to wrench off the side door and was leaning inside, instructing his patient that she could now push.

'Ah!' the woman screamed. 'I don't think I can... Ah!'

'Good girl!' Jason said encouragingly. 'That's brilliant, Megan! I've got baby's head. What a beauty... Now, with the next pain you feel, you can—'

'Ah!'

'You can push again, Megan... And now we're nearly there...'

'How's Pete? Has he come round yet?' Megan asked in a faint voice as she gasped for breath.

Nicky glanced up from suturing Pete's head and viewed the delivery scene taking place on the back seat. Jason, she could see, was completely soaked with rain and sweat as he struggled to deliver the baby.

'Pete hasn't come round yet, Megan,' she said gently. 'But I'm hoping he soon will.'

'Me, too, because— Ah!'

'Well done!' Jason said. 'Just look at this gorgeous little boy you've produced, Megan. Did you ever see such a wonderful sight?'

'Oh, Doctor, you're wonderful!' the happy but exhausted mother said, clutching the newborn baby which Jason had wrapped in his shirt.

Nicky hadn't been able to help but be amused when she'd seen him whipping off his anorak, tearing at his shirt and wrapping the slippery infant inside it. He looked so incongruous now with his anorak gaping open at the front to reveal a bare, damp and, she had to admit it, very sexy, hairy chest.

She felt a pang of something akin to a sensual shiver running down her spine. She remembered how she'd been turned on by him at that dinner party. Looking at him now, she wished fervently that circumstances had been different and the events of the following months hadn't taken place.

Before the dinner party, she'd had no idea that Sue and Jason had been having an affair. When he'd arrived at the flat that evening it had seemed as if they'd simply been lifelong, platonic friends with a more or less brother-and-sister relationship. But what Nicky really couldn't understand was why, when Sue had become pregnant, Jason been so adamant that she had to have a termination even though she would have been happy to have had the baby if Jason hadn't refused to have anything more to do with her.

He'd told Sue that children were a sign of commitment that he wasn't willing to make. Nicky remembered how Sue had sobbed when she'd told her how heartless Jason had been when he'd said this. The memory of the awful times when she'd had to comfort her distraught friend after the pregnancy had been terminated still lingered.

Anyone who didn't know what he was really like would assume that he would make the perfect father. Even she could be taken in again if she suspended judgement. But, no! Thinking back to the agonies that Sue had suffered because of him, she would have to harden her heart.

Quickly remembering that she was supposed to be in a state of truce for the duration of this emergency, she leaned across her still unconscious patient and touched Jason's arm.

'Well done, Jason, and well done, Megan!'

'Oh, what a lovely name, Doctor Jason,' the happy mother said. 'Do you mind if I call my baby Jason?'

Jason smiled. 'Mind? I'd be delighted! I haven't got any children of my own—yet—so it will be great to know I've got a namesake.'

He turned to look at Nicky, who had frozen at his words, and his expression changed. She realised she was still holding onto the sleeve of his anorak.

Quickly she straightened up outside the car, tugging at the hood of the anorak to give some protection to her already soaking hair. Suddenly a faint groan came from the unconscious driver. Leaning back inside the car, she clasped his hand.

'Pete, can you hear me? Pete, I'm Nicky. I'm a doctor and I want to help you. Can you...?'

The bewildered man was opening his eyes, staring

through the shattered windscreen in front of him in a highly perplexed manner.

'I've got to get to hospital,' he murmured. 'My wife's having a baby.'

'Everything's OK, Pete,' Nicky said soothingly. 'Your wife's had a lovely little boy and the emergency services are on their way... There! Can you hear them?'

Her spirits rose as she heard the distinctive sound of an ambulance coming down the hill.

'You say the baby's here? But how...?'

Jason leaned across and held the now squalling infant in front of his father. 'Isn't he a beauty?'

'We're going to call him Jason, love,' Megan said, 'after this wonderful doctor here.'

A slow smile spread across Pete's face. 'Well, I'll be damned. The little fella looks just like my old dad, all wrinkled up and bald and sounding off about nothing in particular. Don't you think so, Megan? I reckon the girls will be dead chuffed with their little brother.'

'He'll get spoiled rotten!' Megan said happily. 'We've got two girls at home with their grandma and they really wanted a little brother to play with.'

The sight of two ambulances pulling up in the gathering gloom was a great relief. Nicky had already gone across to check on Harry and tell him that he was in safe hands.

'I feel dead woozy now, Doctor,' Harry said. 'It's a bit like when I've had six pints on a Friday night. Can I have another of those injections?'

Nicky smiled. 'Not at the moment, Harry. Later on, when you get to hospital, they'll give you something else to keep you comfortable.'

'How's the driver, Doctor?' a paramedic called up to Nicky as she jumped lightly back down again, ripping a bit more from the tear in the cloth.

'Bearing up, but he needs attention as soon as possible. I gave him an intramuscular injection of pethidine, fifty milligrams, about half an hour ago. From the unnatural angle of the lower right leg, I would say he's probably sustained a fracture or fractures of the tibia and or the fibula. The leg will need splinting before he's moved, of course. His name's Harry and he's been very brave so—'

'Don't you worry, Doctor. We'll give him lots of tender loving care. How're you doing, Harry?' he hollered. 'We'll have you out in a jiffy.'

Nicky was already helping to make Megan comfortable in the first ambulance. Pete had been stretchered inside and he was staring, in a dazed condition, up at the roof.

'What I can't figure out, Megan, is how you managed to produce our baby in the back of the car,' Pete mumbled.

'Well, it wasn't easy, but Doctor Jason was fantastic. I couldn't have done it without him.'

'Yes, you could.' Jason appeared suddenly, having finished helping the other paramedics to stretcher Harry inside the second ambulance. 'When it's time for a baby to arrive, Mother Nature takes over. There can sometimes be complications, of course, but in your case it was a straightforward delivery.'

'As easy as shelling peas,' Pete muttered.

'Depends who's doing the shelling!' Megan retorted. 'You can have the next one and I'll do the driving!'

'Nicky, would you like to go in this ambulance with our patients?' Jason said quietly. 'I'll drive along behind and give you a lift back to Highdale when we've handed them all over to the medical staff at Moortown General.'

'Sure!' It was amazing how she was allowing herself to go along with Jason taking charge. Well, someone had to take the lead and Jason was definitely leadership material. Definitely the strong, authoritative type.

The thought flashed, unbidden and unwanted, into her mind that Sue must have been putty in his hands! Years younger than Jason, and of a malleable nature, she would have gone along with all of his suggestions whether she liked them or not.

The doors of the ambulance clanged to and Nicky gave all her attention to her patients, helped by the paramedics. They were swaying up the hill now, rain still pattering relentlessly on the roof. She glanced down at her trousers. They were spattered with mud, completely soaked and the cloth was torn from knee to ankle on one of the legs.

'Looks like you had a ripping time, Doctor!' one of the paramedics quipped.

Nicky laughed. 'You can say that again! There I was, minding my own business at a children's birthday party when, wham, bang, I find myself in the middle of an emergency. And I don't even start work here until tomorrow.'

'Are you one of the new doctors at Highdale Practice?' the paramedic asked.

'Yes. I'm Nicky Devlin and the other doctor is Jason Carmichael.'

'We heard you were coming. You'll like working there. There's a nice warm feeling about the Highdale Practice. I never mind going up there to pick up a patient. Everybody's so friendly.'

Nicky found herself hoping that nothing would change when she and Jason had to work at Highdale Practice together! But, then, she reflected, they'd been supportive with each other just now. There hadn't been any problems so maybe things would work out professionally at least.

Jason was hurrying inside the hospital as Nicky came down the corridor after handing over her patients to the Moortown General Hospital medical staff.

'I couldn't get to you. The police were already here and insisted on asking so many questions that—'

She noticed how breathless he was. 'That's OK. I've only just finished settling the three of them with the appropriate staff. You look like a drowned rat!'

He grinned. 'Thanks very much! Have you taken a look at yourself? I like the latest ripped trouser detail. Is that a new fashion?'

Nicky laughed, in spite of her discomfort. 'It's all the rage in Paris on the catwalk.'

A couple of young female patients were giggling as they walked past.

'We'd better move on,' Jason said. 'We're attracting the most curious glances.'

His hand was under her wet sleeve. She tried not to object to the fact that this was Jason Carmichael who was escorting her out through the front doors of Accident and Emergency. A fragile rapport had built up between them as they'd worked together. She wasn't about to break it just because their real work was finished. For the moment she would cruise along with this nice, warm, friendly feeling and pretend she'd only just met this very personable doctor and didn't know anything at all about his past.

She promised herself that later, much later, she would find the opportunity to delve into his doubtful past. But for the moment she felt emotionally and physically drained and she needed a period of relaxation to recover her equilibrium.

'Where are you living?' he asked, as he closed the passenger door on her and went round to climb in the driver's seat of his black sports car.

Nicky leaned back against the comfortable leather seat, revelling in the feeling of luxury that the extravagantly appointed interior of the car exuded.

'I've got a little house along the main street of Highdale village. I'm renting it from Patricia and Adam. Apparently Patricia lived there before she married Adam. It feels very cosy but I need to arrange my own possessions around the place before it becomes home, even though it feels like a happy house.'

'It should be a happy house. Patricia and Adam had a happy romance, I believe.'

He paused at the hospital entrance to wait until the two cars in front of him could turn out into the road. Nicky had the distinct feeling that he was watching her. She turned to look at him and saw that the expression in his eyes seemed warm and friendly.

She swallowed hard. 'Yes, I heard they were a very romantic couple. And you've only got to look at them to see the romance is still there, even though they've got all those children to look after.'

Jason was looking back at the road again, turning the wheel to move into the road. 'Amazing, really! When I think of all the sad marriages I've known, they really are exceptional. But, as you say, the romance is still obviously there between Patricia and Adam. Often it disappears when the parents get caught up in the day-to-day commitment of looking after children. But I'm not an expert on the subject.'

'You can say that again!' Nicky muttered under her breath, suddenly unable to quell her rising resentment, despite her earlier resolve to keep her personal feelings out of it for the time being.

'Sorry—what did you say?'

'Nothing!' She looked out of the passenger window at the Moortown traffic. They were in the middle of the rush hour now. People clutching umbrellas were hurrying to catch buses or trying to hail taxis.

'And Jane and Richard are another lucky couple,' Jason continued. 'Even with a two-year-old and Jane's complicated pregnancy, you can see she's very much in love with Richard. Didn't you notice that when you came for interview?'

'I did notice,' Nicky said quietly. 'I can't help wondering if they're the exceptions to the general rule.'

'You could be right. I suppose. As an old bachelor I can't really speak from experience. I've always avoided taking on commitments.'

Well, that was certainly true, but why was he admitting it? Didn't he know Sue had told her everything? Obviously not!

Maybe she could probe deeper. 'But even if you've never been married, you must have had some...er...meaningful relationships that might have led to...'

'Oh, I've had a couple of meaningful relationships, as you put it,' he said wryly. 'I almost got married once but I decided it was too risky.'

Nicky held her breath for a few seconds, not daring to say anything for fear of interrupting his revelations. But none were forthcoming.

'Risky?' she asked after a few seconds when neither of them spoke. 'In what way?'

'I found out that my girlfriend was the same type as...as someone in my past, someone I was trying to forget so... Look, I don't want to go into it.'

His voice was firm but she wasn't intimidated. She had no idea if he was speaking about Sue. Had it been Sue who'd been like this mysterious person in the past that he'd been trying to forget?

'Were there...er...children involved...in your relationship, I mean?' The intrusive question was out before she could stop herself.

'Children?' He sounded wounded. 'I told you, I've never been married. Children would have involved marriage or a serious long term relationship. This girl was simply my girlfriend for a short time. The relationship wasn't going anywhere so I opted out.'

Nicky looked out of the window again. They had escaped the town and were climbing the hill that led to Highdale. She was completely confused and decided to let it go for the moment. Maybe he'd been talking about Sue, maybe he hadn't, but this was neither the time nor the place to go into a deep interrogation.

If he had been talking about Sue, he obviously didn't know that she herself was aware of what had happened. She would have to enlighten him sooner rather than later. This state of affairs couldn't continue. But, watching him gripping the wheel that led to the top of the hill overlooking Highdale, she knew this wasn't the right moment to give him a nasty shock.

They were cruising down the steep hill now. Rivulets of rainwater tumbled down each side of the road, making it dangerously narrow. At times they had to pull over into the newly formed stream to allow the upward driving traffic to use the whole of the road. The windscreen wipers crossed and recrossed rapidly, doing their best to cope with the torrential rain.

'You live on the main street, you say?'

They were nearing Highdale. The river running through the village was brown and swollen to the point that it looked as if it might burst its banks. Sandbags were stacked in huge piles at the edge of the village and volunteers were busily building sandbag walls in front of the houses.

Jason frowned and stopped the car, leaning through the side window to speak to a policeman who seemed to be supervising the operation from the middle of the road.

'Highdale's on flood alert, sir,' the policeman shouted above the noise of the rushing river and the babble of voices from the worried villagers. 'You can't go into the village.'

Nicky leaned across Jason to speak through the open window. 'But I'm a resident, officer.'

'Doesn't matter if you're the Queen of England, madam, you'll have to find somewhere else to sleep tonight. If you're stuck, they've opened up the school, just up the hill there. They'll find you a hot meal and some blankets to bed down for the night.'

For a couple of seconds she remained still until she realised that she was leaning across Jason's chest. The Velcro fastening on his anorak had worked loose and she was in close contact with his bare skin.

'Ooh, sorry!' She began to extricate herself from her embarrassing position but Jason put his hands on her shoulders.

'Why be sorry? I don't mind. It's rather nice to be snuggling up to an auburn-haired beauty in the middle of a crisis like this. I hope you realise you're homeless for the moment and we'll have to work out what we're going to do about it.'

To her shock and surprise, his voice was husky, decidedly sexy as he looked down at her. His eyes were warm, tender almost, and she caught a glimpse of the intense interest he'd shown in her on that first evening. In spite of the fact that she'd stood him up, he was making it obvious that he still fancied her. Thinking of Sue, Nicky felt uncontrollable anger welling up inside her.

But at that moment she had a blinding flash of inspiration. She realised how she could get even with this man for the brutal, heartless way he'd treated her flatmate.

Maybe she could teach him a lesson in commitment he wouldn't forget in a hurry!

Looking back to their first evening together, Jason had made it obvious that he'd felt a deep attraction towards her. If this feeling for her was still there—and all the signs at the moment pointed to the fact that it was—then she could go along with it, only to really hurt him when she broke up their pseudo-relationship. It was no more than he deserved! And when she got to the point where she told him she didn't want to commit herself, she would also reveal that she knew all about the way he'd treated Sue and that she'd only been pretending to reciprocate his feelings to set him up for a fall.

Could she really go through with it? Remembering Sue's pain, Nicky hardened her heart and took a deep calming breath. She'd ring her flatmate the moment she was alone. 'Will you take me up to Patricia and Adam's? I've got to pick up my car and we ought to let them know what's been happening.'

'I phoned them when I'd spoken to the police and gave them a full report,' he said, reversing the car back along the street before turning into the main road again. 'Patricia's invited us back for supper.'

'Supper sounds great, but I'm going to look like a waterlogged scarecrow in this wet outfit.'

'Patricia will have something she can lend you,' he said, his eyes on the upward road.

Nicky thought about her diminutive colleague. 'I doubt she'll have anything long enough.'

'Tell you what, we'll call into my flat over the old stables at Highdale House. Maria, one of the community nurses, lived there with her husband until she got pregnant and they bought a house. She's left loads of old clothes and I was asked if I'd mind taking them to a charity shop. Haven't got around to it yet so you can take your pick.'

He took his eyes off the road for a brief moment as though to judge her reaction. Nicky happened to be scrutinising him at the time, thinking, in spite of herself, what a helpful man Jason Carmichael could be if he felt that way inclined. She felt an embarrassing flush spreading over her cheeks as he caught her weighing him up.

'Well, what do you say?' His eyes were back on the road. They were nearing the Highdale Practice.

She smiled. 'Beggars can't be choosers. As I'm homeless and with not a stitch to wear, I'll take up your kind offer.'

'Seems to make sense,' he said evenly. 'I've also got to call in and change.'

Nicky followed Jason up the ancient stone outside staircase that led to the flat above the old stables at Highdale House.

Jason turned the large iron key in the old lock. 'Bags of atmosphere but fairly basic.' He led the way inside.

'Oh, it's great!' She walked across the worn flagstones of the kitchen-cum-living room. 'I love old buildings!' She peeped through the open door that led off the room she'd just crossed. 'Sorry, that's your bedroom.'

She turned back into the room. He was standing right behind her and she found herself looking up into his eyes.

'That's OK. The shower room's through the bedroom. Water's hot if you want to indulge yourself after your ordeal.' He grinned. 'There's a fair bit of mud still lingering.'

He reached forward and touched the side of her cheek. 'Here, for instance. Can't think how it got there.'

Nicky raised her hand to the place he was touching. Her hand met his and she pulled it hastily away. What kind of power did this man have? He was a dangerous man. Sue had told her how easily he'd led her on and then dumped her. But the tables had turned. She was the one who would call the shots now. There was no chance that Jason could hurt her feelings because she knew exactly what he was like and she was the one in charge.

'I'd love a shower. Thanks.'

Jason smiled. 'You go ahead. I'll put the kettle on for when you're finished. Tea or coffee?'

His voice was deliberately brisk.

'Coffee, please, black, no sugar.'

'Coming up!'

Nicky went into Jason's bedroom and closed the door firmly behind her. As he'd told her, it was very basic, but it was cosy. Bookshelves lined one wall and a basket chair stood against another beside a huge wardrobe. A minuscule dressing table was jammed up against another wardrobe. 'Compact and cosy' would be an estate agent's description.

She took off her damp outer clothing and sat down on his bed. She retrieved her mobile from her suit pocket and dialled Sue's number. It would be early morning now in Sydney. She hoped Sue was up. Her health had been so precarious when she'd last seen her that—

'Hi, Sue? It's Nicky.' She kept her voice low just in case.

There was a slight pause. 'I wondered when you would phone.'

'I was thinking the same about you. Didn't you get my letter with the new number?'

'Yes, I did. Sorry I haven't got around to replying but you know what I'm like. What on earth made you go up to Yorkshire, Nicky?'

'I needed a change from London.' It would take too long to go into details on an expensive call! 'I wanted to tell you, I've met up with Jason Carmichael again. He's actually going to work here at the same surgery and—'

Over the clear line Nicky heard Sue's gasp of horror. 'Sue, are you OK?'

'It came as a bit of a shock, that's all. I hadn't expected...' Sue's voice trailed away.

'Don't worry, Sue, I understand,' Nicky continued briskly. 'I've decided to teach him a lesson for what he did to you. He seems interested in having a relationship with me so I'm pretending to go along with it. As soon as he seems hooked, I'm going to dump him, but not before I've told him I only did it so I could get revenge for the awful way he treated you. What do you think?'

There was a long pause before Sue replied quietly, 'Seems like a good plan. Are you sure you can handle it?'

Nicky tried to banish her apprehension. 'Of course. But, Sue, I'm doing this for you. I thought you would be really pleased.'

'Yes, yes, I am' There was a little more animation in Sue's voice now. 'Serves him right. Again, it was a shock. Yes, go for it and...and let me know how you get on.'

'I will. After all the suffering Jason put you through, he's got to realise he can't go around treating people like—'

'Nicky, I've got to go.' Sue had lowered her voice. 'I can hear Mum coming and she doesn't know anything about the baby or—'

The line went dead. Nicky switched off her mobile and thought. Sue had been very subdued. It was obvious she hadn't fully recovered. It would take Sue a long time to recover after the suffering she'd gone through.

It made Nicky all the more determined to carry out her plan. Sue would feel better when she knew that justice had been done.

Suddenly there was movement under the rumpled navy and white duvet and she gave a cry of surprise. A black and white cat was crawling out sleepily from the depths of the cover, eyeing her warily.

'Oh, you beautiful cat! Puss, puss puss.' She smiled and held out her hand.

'I think you must have found Miriam,' Jason called from the other room. 'She comes with the flat. Jane tried to move her down to Fellside when she left Highdale House but she always comes back to her first home. She won't budge from the place where she was born.'

'Poor Miriam, she's only got three legs.' Nicky sat down on the bed and began stroking the purring cat.

'She got caught in a trap. Jane had to amputate the mangled leg. It doesn't seem to worry her. You've been a long time. Have you found out how to work the shower yet?'

There were footsteps crossing the outer room. Surely he wasn't going to come in when she was stripped down to her bra and pants! Nicky jumped up from the bed and hurried into the shower room, closing the door behind her. She'd left her wet anorak, suit and blouse on the floor of Jason's bedroom. Stripping off her undies, she stepped into the shower and turned on the tap.

As the hot water cascaded over her she let out a sigh of relief. It was bliss to be really warm again. The drowned-rat feeling vanished down the plughole and she felt like a person again. Her hair couldn't get any wetter. She reached for the bottle of shampoo sitting beside the soap. Jason wouldn't mind—she hoped. Didn't matter if he did! Mmm...that felt so good. What was the scent? Pine maybe, or cedar—something intensely masculine.

Turning off the tap, she stepped out of the cubicle and looked around for a towel. It was only a couple of steps to a shelf where there was a huge pile. She could hear Miriam miaowing plaintively from the bedroom. She probably wanted to be let out.

Enveloped in a large, white, fluffy towel, she towel-dried her long hair before going back into the bedroom. Jason was standing beside the bed, tying the knot on a black towelling robe.

He looked up in alarm. 'Sorry! I meant to be out of here before you'd finished. I opened the door to let Miriam into the kitchen and decided I just couldn't bear my wet clothes any longer.'

Their eyes met. She could feel her heart beating as she put one hand up to check that the towel was still held in place under her arms. Her damp auburn hair hung seductively loose over her shoulders. She wished she'd tied it in a severe knot or wrapped it in a towel. She felt intensely vulnerable.

'It's great to feel warm and dry again, isn't it?' she said quickly.

He moved towards her. 'Your hair looks beautiful when you don't tie it back.'

Jason put out a hand and touched one of the strands. Nicky stood absolutely still, knowing she should move away but reluctantly enjoying Jason's close proximity. She'd felt attracted to him the first time she'd met him, and therein lay the danger...

She could feel an overwhelming desire deep down inside her to move into a more physical zone. No, she mustn't get too carried away, mustn't mistake her feelings of desire for the real thing. Keep a clear head and don't get involved... Her pulses were beginning to race. Wrapped only in a towel, her skin vibrant from the pulsating shower, she purposely moved towards him.

From the tender look in his eyes, it seemed to her that he sensed the magnetic current of pure desire running between them. She felt herself breathing more rapidly as she looked at his athletic body encased only in that black, sexy robe. Her hands shook slightly as they moved across to lightly touch the collar of the robe.

It was an invitation. She knew it and Jason recognised the signal as he pulled her gently into his arms. He looked down at her, his eyes searching her face for any sign of rejection. She felt as if she were under the influence of a magic spell. She tried to tell herself that this experience was all part of her plan, that she was simply putting on a good show. But at that moment she knew it wasn't that simple.

He hesitated for only a second before his lips claimed hers and with that, Nicky was lost. She couldn't stifle the sigh that escaped. She recognised that this was how she'd felt the last time she'd been in the arms of this captivating man. It was as if the intervening events were all a myth and now, here in his arms, she allowed only her initial attraction towards him to have any sway as she gave herself up to the primeval longings that had tortured her on that first meeting.

His hands were caressing her, oh, so gently, so soothingly, igniting the dormant passions that she'd held in check when she'd first met him. She raised her hands to his face. The eyes were tender, almost loving, as if making love with each other was the most natural thing in the world. It was some kind of destiny that she'd been driven towards since Jason had walked into her life. She didn't understand it and didn't want to question it until later... much later...when they'd consummated their passion.

But even as Nicky melted into his embrace, revelling in the feel of Jason's lips against hers, the still small voice of reason reminded her that she was already becoming too involved. Keeping Jason's interest in her was essential if she was to succeed in her plan but she mustn't allow herself to get carried away—as she had just done.

The bedside phone was ringing. He drew back and reached for it. 'Jason Carmichael.'

Her emotions were in turmoil as she watched him. This timely interruption had given her the opportunity to come to her senses and resist the sensual temptations that had surged through her. She tried to tell herself that she had only been acting out a part but she knew it had been more than that. She had been overwhelmed by the attraction she'd felt towards him.

She noticed that his voice was husky and she felt again the ripples of desire running through her body, that treacherous body that had led her completely astray.

'Hi, Patricia! Yes, I came back here to change. Nicky's with me...she needed to change too. We were absolutely soaked so... I'm going to give her the run of Maria's cast-offs... Sure! Half an hour.'

He put the phone down, turned to look at her and smiled regretfully.

'Patricia wants us there as soon as we can make it.'

Nicky nodded, her face flaming as she clutched her towel to her breasts.

'Let me find you a robe and then you can take your pick of Maria's clothes.'

He padded barefoot to the smaller of the two wardrobes. As he flung open the doors, she couldn't help but remember the way his lips had felt against hers as they'd kissed. It had been an out-of-this-world experience, but it wasn't one she should allow to happen again. The emotions involved were too difficult to control. Still pulsating from the joy of being held in Jason's arms, she realised she was already getting in too deep.

She pulled on the voluminous cotton kaftan he'd foraged

from the depths of the wardrobe. Standing beside him, Nicky was intensely aware that he was watching her as she riffled through the selection of garments. He put his hands on her shoulders and turned her gently towards him, his eyes searching her face.

He gathered her into his arms and she found him impossible to resist as his sensual lips claimed hers once more. His kiss was tender but as his passion deepened she found the strength to pull herself away. What had been intended as a mere game was in danger of becoming a situation out of control.

'We really ought to go,' she said breathlessly, running a hand through her tangled hair, still slightly damp from the shower.

The expression in his eyes showed that she'd hurt his feelings. She should have felt pleased that she'd reached him in this way, that, despite her own fears, maybe her plan would succeed.

But she didn't.

CHAPTER THREE

NICKY stared out of her consulting room window as she waited for her patient to undress behind the curtains she'd drawn around the examination couch. It seemed longer than a week since that mad, magic moment with Jason. She couldn't believe even now that she could have abandoned all her sensible judgement long enough to kiss Jason in that way. It would be difficult to convince him that she'd only been setting him up for a fall!

Her obvious enjoyment, her total involvement, her utter abandonment...! She swallowed hard as she reviewed her behaviour. It was as if she'd been controlled by some magic spell. And even thinking about him now, hearing his subdued voice from the next room, was awakening shivers of desire inside her. She gave herself a mental shake as she watched the clouds racing along in the pale blue October sky. She must never let herself get carried away like that again! Not with Jason.

A tiny little voice inside her head had been plaguing her ever since. The man who'd held her so tenderly in his arms had seemed utterly alien to the man who'd ruined Sue's life. Had Sue painted too wicked a portrait of him? Could some of the blame for the tragedy of Sue's affair lie partly with Sue and not completely with Jason? Could she trust Sue enough to believe the awful story that she'd told her?

She gave a shiver as she reflected that she'd constantly mulled over such a possibility but had been unable to come up with a definite answer. Sue had never lied to her in the short time they'd shared a flat together. But she had sounded so strange on the phone. Why should she lie about such a sensitive subject? No, she had to remember that, however charming Jason might seem, he was capable of inflicting hurt on someone of a trusting nature.

Suddenly disgusted with herself for allowing one kiss to cause her to question Sue's integrity, Nicky focused her thoughts. She'd already come this far in her plan to bring him down. The fact that she'd enjoyed encouraging his attraction towards her shouldn't stop her from continuing her desire to teach him a lesson. The more he wanted her, the more he would suffer when she told him she'd set him up. That was what she wanted, wasn't it?

Reviewed in the cold light of day, it seemed heartless, but heartlessly was exactly how he'd behaved towards Sue and therefore somebody had to teach him a lesson. He had to be shown how awful it was to trifle with someone's affections.

Nicky made a conscious effort to ban the intrusive thoughts from her mind as she watched the picturesque hills that rolled down towards the valley beyond her window. The weather, as if to make recompense for the storm damage a week ago, had turned mild and dry. The level of Highdale Beck had subsided and was now back to normal. She'd been relieved that she'd only been homeless for one night and there had been no flooding across the street into her little house after all. Patricia and Adam had, very kindly, insisted she stay the night at Greystones after the supper party on that fateful evening.

She remembered how she'd surveyed the long table, surrounded by her new friends and colleagues in the ornate dining room, feeling decidedly strange in her borrowed dress. It was a voluminous affair which she'd cinched in at the waist with one of Jason's leather belts, wrapped around twice! Jason had laughed when he'd first seen her but had told her that she still looked very attractive and intensely desirable.

That had been the point at which she'd had to remind herself not to get carried away again.

They'd both been positively cool with each other on the short car journey to Greystones. It was as if they had both been rehearsing their expected role of newly introduced, professional colleagues. They'd both given profuse apologies for turning up so late.

Patricia had been the perfect hostess, thanking them for dealing with the emergency and allowing her and Adam to keep Emma's birthday party going. It had seemed bizarre that Patricia should have put Jason at the other end of the table from Nicky. She'd taken her on one side and whispered that she'd noticed there had been a little tension between her and Jason when they'd arrived at the birthday party earlier in the day. Had they been able to work together at the scene of the crash without too many problems?

Nicky assured her hostess that in spite of their initial antipathy towards each other they'd coped well in a professional situation. If Patricia only knew!

She found her eyes straying down the table towards where Jason was talking animatedly with Jane and Richard. Beside her, Adam proved to be an amusing conversationalist, but her mind was still on the unreal events that had preceded the supper party. She only gave half her attention to what was going on around her.

Was it her imagination, or had Jason been avoiding her during the past week? They'd both been terribly busy, settling into their new jobs. She simply hadn't had time to rethink her strategy towards him. Teaching him a lesson was going to be a difficult task fraught with unforeseen dangers, the most treacherous of which were her own emotions and desires.

She remembered how, at the end of the supper party, Jason had gone away, barely acknowledging her in his collective, 'Goodnight, everybody!'

Nicky had realised that there had been time to review the situation before she'd had to meet him in a professional capacity. Patricia's offer of a bedroom for as long as she needed it had been a great relief because she'd known she wouldn't have trusted herself to have gone back to Jason's flat with him that evening.

'I'm ready, Doctor.'

Nicky came back to the present as she went across, moved inside the curtains and gave all her thoughts to her patient. Belinda Turner was thirty-five and, at twenty-two weeks pregnant, she was hoping that this pregnancy wouldn't end like the previous three had done. She lifted her blonde head from the pillow as Nicky went in, her expression weary and resigned.

'I know I've got my monthly check-up in a couple of weeks, Doctor, but I'm getting so nervous, the bigger I get. I've always been OK until about twenty-five weeks and then—'

Mrs Turner broke off as the tears overwhelmed her. Nicky put her arm around the heaving shoulders and held her patient until the sobbing subsided.

'It must have been so awful for you, Belinda,' she said gently. 'Losing three premature babies is just too awful to think about. No wonder you're worried. You were quite right to come in and see us so that we can do a check-up.'

She listened to the baby's heartbeat and asked her patient if she'd like to listen in through the Pinard's stethoscope.

Belinda smiled as she listened. 'I listened like this with all the others.' The smile faded. 'And then, one by one, they all slipped out too early, before they were ready, and they only survived a few hours...'

'Which consultant are you under?' Nicky asked quietly.

'I think he's called Beecham. I haven't actually met him. I always see a different doctor each time.'

An idea was forming inside Nicky's head. She desperately wanted her patient to carry this baby to term.

'Belinda, would you mind if I have a word with my colleague? I'd like a second opinion and Dr Carmichael, who's recently joined the practice, has had a great deal of experience with prenatal care.'

Belinda looked pleased. 'I need as much help as I can get.'

Nicky went back to her desk. It wasn't Jason's expertise she was after so much as the fact that he was a personal friend of James Beecham. Perhaps he could use his influence to put Belinda on the priority list. The reasons for her frequent miscarriages needed to be investigated. She dialled Jason's number on the internal phone.

'Jason...it's Nicky. Are you with a patient?'

'No, not at the moment.' His voice was polite and professional. 'How can I help?'

She lowered her voice. 'Could you come in and look at one of my patients who's had three premature babies? She's a patient of your friend James Beecham and I wondered if you could use your influence to have her investigated more thoroughly. She's desperate to carry this one to term.'

'When did she last miscarry?'

'Seven years ago. And they were living in the Midlands at the time. I don't think the reason for her miscarriages has been investigated.'

There was a slight pause. 'Well, signicant advances have been made in obstetrics and especially in the treatment of patients who've had several miscarriages in the last few years,' he said thoughtfully. 'We may be able to discover the cause if she's willing to spend a lot of time in hospital.'

'I would imagine she would find that a small price to pay.'

'I'm on my way…'

She put down the phone, feeling relieved that they'd been able to conduct a professional discussion without their complicated personal relationship intruding.

Belinda was perfectly happy for Jason to examine her. She watched him with eyes that beseeched him to help her. At the end of the examination, he told her that he would contact James Beecham and, hopefully, she would have an early appointment to see him. He asked if she would be willing to submit to a number of tests and she was adamant that she would do anything if it meant she would produce a healthy child. She'd been planning to rest for the second half of her pregnancy anyway, and if she was under hospital supervision, that would give her peace of mind that everything possible was being done to save her precious baby.

Jason closed the door after their grateful patient had departed and came over to lean against Nicky's desk.

'I have a hunch that James might decide to put in a Shirodkar suture. That's what I would do.'

Nicky sat upright in her chair and watched Jason as he looked down at her. 'I've read about that but never actually met a patient who's been treated that way.'

'It's sometimes used to treat patients with frequent miscarriages. Basically, as you will know from your reading, a special stitch is inserted in the neck of the womb to prevent the baby being expelled before it's due. From the details Belinda gave me just now, it's possible that technique might work for her. I'll go and give James a call now.'

He was halfway to the door.

'Thank you very much,' she said quietly.

Her relief that something was being done to solve her patient's problem turned to concern as she saw him about to return to his own surgery again. This was exactly what it had been like all week—a quick conference about a patient and then a return to their own domains. Off-duty times hadn't seemed to coincide either.

As he took hold of the doorhandle, she switched from her professional mode. 'Jason, hold on a minute.' She swallowed hard. 'Are you free this evening?'

She saw the surprise that registered on his face. 'Yes, I'm free this evening...but, Nicky...' He paused as if searching for the right words. 'I'm not sure it would be a good idea to meet up again, under the circumstances.'

He ran a hand through his dark hair, pulling the wayward strands away from his forehead. 'Last week...it happened...and you probably don't want it to happen again so...'

Nicky felt completely lost by his weird statement. Why did he presume *she* wouldn't want it to happen again?

She cleared her throat. 'I simply thought we could have a pleasant evening together. I'll cook supper and we'll listen to some music. You look as if you need to relax, so I insist you take some time out.'

He smiled, but his eyes held that slightly mocking expression that alarmed her. '"Insist" is a very strong word. What a forceful, independent girl you are, Nicky! Sue told me all about you but I hadn't realised just what a powerful woman you really are.'

The mention of Sue galvanised her. If he'd somehow formed the opinion that she was a bossy woman then that's how she would behave! 'Eight o' clock at my place. Number five, Front Street.'

He pulled himself to his full height again, the smile still lingering on his lips. 'I'll be there.'

Her thoughts were in turmoil as she watched him leaving her consulting room. She wondered how she'd had the nerve to give him such a bold invitation. After the way she'd practically seduced him last week, it was no wonder he'd formed the opinion that she was forward! But what had Sue told him that made him think he understood her better than he really did?

Jason was holding the bottle of wine in front of him as if it were some kind of shield.

'Peace offering,' he said, with a wide, boyish grin.

Nicky held the front door open and smiled.

'I wasn't aware that we were at war.'

'I'm not used to fierce, bossy women.'

Jason's eyes were alight with amusement, so she took it that he was still joking. He was wearing jeans and a dark blue fisherman's jersey. She thought he looked very sexy with his hair tumbled over his forehead, and those emerald green eyes, staring straight at her, were decidedly unnerving.

'Welcome to Devlin Castle!' She glanced outside at his conspicuous car parked in front of her house. That would set the neighbours talking!

Nicky turned and led the way along the narrow, flag-stoned passage, past the tiny sitting room to the kitchen. 'Thank you for the wine. I think I've got a corkscrew somewhere…'

She rummaged in one of the kitchen drawers. Patricia had left most of the kitchen utensils she needed but she wasn't sure of a corkscrew. Her fingers were trembling slightly as she turned over numerous implements. She felt intensely nervous, overwhelmingly aware that Jason was standing right behind her, towering above her.

'Damn!' She pulled her index finger up to her mouth and sucked on the newly pierced skin. 'I didn't know that sharp knife was lurking at the back of the drawer.'

'Here, let me have a look.'

He put his hands on her shoulders and gently turned her around so that she was facing him much closer than she'd planned at this early stage of the evening.

'Trust me, I'm a doctor,' Jason quipped, and Nicky smiled back at him as she felt herself relaxing. 'That's quite a deep cut.'

He held her finger under the cold tap. 'Have you got something we can bind your finger with or shall I call out the ambulance?'

She laughed. 'I've got a roll of sticky plaster in that cupboard.'

They sat together at the kitchen table as he bound up her finger. She watched his long tapering fingers lingering over hers and had to suppress a shiver as the memories of that passionate kiss forced themselves upon her.

'I'd better open the wine as you're now incapacitated,' he said, rising to his feet. Searching another drawer more cautiously, he produced a corkscrew and proceeded to do the honours.

He poured the wine and held out a glass towards her. Nicky looked up from leaning over the oven, her face flushed with the heat rising from the casserole she was holding with both hands.

'Can you put the glass down on the table for me?'

'Here, let me take the casserole.' Jason picked up a thick oven cloth and removed the dish from her hands.

Their hands touched in the manoeuvre involved and she felt her face flush even more as she reflected that it was strange how you could kiss someone in the heat of the moment and yet still feel intensely shy when you met in everyday situations afterwards.

He placed the wineglass in her hand and insisted she sit down again at the table.

'You're probably still suffering from shock,' he said, with mock gravity. 'Maybe I should take your temperature.'

She laughed again as she watched Jason across the table. She found herself wishing with all her heart that he would come up with some good explanation about his dealings with Sue because it would be so wonderful to be able to have a normal relationship with him. But as quickly as the thought arose she banished it. She knew the facts. She'd seen the damage he'd inflicted on Sue. She would serve the supper, spend an hour or so listening to music and chatting in a platonic way before making it clear that he should be on his way.

Nicky had covered the kitchen table with a red and white gingham cloth she'd found in the linen drawer in the sitting room. There were napkins to match. Suddenly feeling festive, she reached across, opened the cupboard under the sink and produced a candle in an ancient metal candleholder which she placed in the middle of the table.

Jason jumped to his feet and brought the box of matches from the side of the old fashioned gas cooker.

'Quite an occasion!' he said as he lit the candle before leaning back in his chair and looking across the table at Nicky. 'Did you make this casserole yourself? I mean, it's not prepacked, chilled, ready prepared…'

She grinned. 'It's only my tried and tested chicken casserole, quick version. Called in at the village shop on my way home and bought a couple of chicken breasts, some mushrooms and a tin of their spicy chicken sauce. Add some mashed potatoes…' She paused to spoon some on to his plate. 'And stir all the ingredients together with a couple of hungry doctors.'

'It's delicious! Where did you learn to cook like this?'

'Oh, this is just survival cooking. I taught myself in a bedsit during medical school and afterwards. I bought myself a tiny little portable oven, just big enough for a small casserole and I used to carry it around from bedsit to bedsit. It's still waiting to be unpacked in a box somewhere. I've never had a real grown-up oven like this one to play with.'

He put down his fork. 'But wasn't your mother a good cook?'

'Mum's hopeless at cooking! When she was travelling with my dad overseas they always had a cook and when they came home on leave we used to live off prepared meals or go out to restaurants. My dad was in the army and—why are you looking so puzzled?'

'Sue told me your mother was a downtrodden housewife. You had very little money at home and your mother deeply regretted ever getting married. Your father wouldn't let her go out to work and she'd advised you never to get married because it was sheer slavery.'

Nicky leaned against the back of her chair and stared at Jason as he was telling her this incredible make-believe story.

'And you believed her?'

'Well, of course I did! It's a perfectly plausible story. I've known families like that. Besides, I'd only met you once so how was I to know otherwise? I've known Sue since she was a child living in the same village. Our parents were friends and I've never doubted anything she told me before.'

'But when did she tell you this?'

He looked uncomfortable. 'It was towards the end of the dinner party. Just before she went off to bed and left you to play hostess. She called me into the kitchen. I thought she needed help with the coffee or something but...' Jason paused, watching her face, carefully. 'You and I had just been talking about how we both loved the theatre and I'd told you to stay right there until I got back.'

'I remember,' she said quietly.

She'd sat watching the door to the kitchen, longing for his return. Soon after he'd come back to his place, Sue had wandered in, obviously the worse for drinking too much wine, and that had been when she'd agreed to take over so that Sue could go to bed.

'Sue must have been drunk when she told you that,' Nicky said lightly. 'Her brain must have been totally addled.'

But she couldn't help doubts about Sue from tumbling into her head. Maybe she would give her another call. After all, she was doing all this for Sue. Enjoyable as the experience of being with Jason was proving to be, it wasn't something she would have chosen to do if she hadn't been trying to get back at him.

She got up from the table and went over to the window. He followed her and put his hands on her shoulders, holding her back against his chest. She could feel the steady rhythm of his breathing and it helped to calm her as she stared out into the darkened garden. The outlines of the large earthenware plant pots stood out in the eerie light of the moon, which had just appeared from behind a cloud. A stray cat shot across the gravel, scattering the tiny stones onto the narrow path.

Suddenly, the doubts became stronger. If Sue could make up a fantasy story like this about her, what else could she have lied about? But Sue's pregnancy had been a fact. She'd accompanied her flatmate to the clinic where a surgeon had removed the ten-week-old foetus. That had been real enough and so had the traumatic weeks of agony and self-recrimination that Sue had suffered afterwards, crying and screaming Jason's name...

Slowly, she turned to look up into Jason's eyes. 'What else did Sue tell you about me?'

His hands still held her lightly by the shoulders. 'Nothing much. I think she was just rambling.'

Nicky moved away so that she was loosened from his grip. She knew she had to distance herself from Jason if she was to think coherently.

'You're probably right.'

She walked back to the table, picking up her wineglass and taking a sip. The smooth liquid soothed her jangled nerves. He joined her at the table, toying with his fork.

Suddenly he put it down on the side of his plate and faced her across the table.

'And whilst we're on the subject of Sue's dinner party, I can't help wondering why you didn't turn up for our date.'

She stared at him, her mind suddenly in turmoil. She could come clean now and tell him she knew everything, that she couldn't possibly have moved in on Sue's boyfriend, that she knew all about the terminated pregnancy.

But it was too soon to let him off the hook. She had to keep the charade going a little while longer so as to gain maximum effect. She couldn't give up now.

Nicky forced a smile on to her face. 'Oh, something came up, I think. Yes, I remember now, I had to take on an extra duty at the surgery that evening and by the time I'd finished...'

He raised an eyebrow mockingly. 'And all the phone lines were down?'

'I lost your phone number.'

'You're a rotten liar! Why not just say you'd had second thoughts? That was why you put the phone down on me, wasn't it?'

It was so difficult not to blurt out the truth! But she stuck to her guns. 'I really don't remember. It was a very busy time and it's ages ago.'

'And it meant nothing to you, did it?' he said quietly. 'I should have known.'

Nicky looked at him, hearing the pathos in his voice. He'd obviously been hurt before.

He narrowed his eyes. 'I must admit, I was surprised by the warm way you reacted last week. I hadn't expected you to—'

'Look, can't we forget that we met before and have a new start?'

Jason smiled. 'I'd like that very much.'

In spite of herself, her heart turned over for him. He had a little-boy-lost look that tore at her heartstrings. This was a man she was trying to set up for his past misdemeanours but he looked as if he wasn't capable of hurting a fly. And the feelings she was having towards him right now were anything but vindictive.

Slowly, he stood up and came round the table to pull her to her feet so that he could fold her into his arms. She should have resisted but she didn't. She felt the need for the comfort of his embrace, quite apart from the sensual thrill that simmered through her when she was held against his hard, virile body again.

'I'm glad we can start again,' he said huskily.

Nicky looked up into his deeply sincere eyes and realised how much she wanted to trust him.

'I'm going to phone Sue soon, just to check she's OK,' she said quickly, pulling herself away. It was so important now to get the facts straight before she got in deeper than she was now. 'She's been feeling tired and run down, which was why she went out to Australia to stay with her parents.'

'I've got her parents' number, I think,' he said quietly. He was already thumbing through a leather-bound notebook. 'Sue's mother gave me the number a couple of years ago when they retired out there... Yes, here it is. I'd like to check it's still the same one.'

Nicky reached for her mobile phone and they compared notes.

'Yes, that's correct,' she said quietly.

'I thought Sue was still in London until you told me she'd gone to Australia,' Jason said slowly. 'I've been so busy I hadn't given her a thought. Often, I didn't see her for ages and then she would phone up and invite me to go and see her on stage if she had a small part at the theatre.'

Nicky swallowed hard. Either he was a very good actor or Sue had misled her.

'Yes, she was always keen to invite friends when she was acting,' she said in a matter-of-fact voice. 'But her agent hadn't found anything for her for months. She'd been resting for quite a while, as they say in the acting profession, and she was getting very bored, as I recall.'

All this emotional trauma was getting to her. She felt unable to take any more for the moment and she deliberately moved away from him.

'Look, let's go and sit in the sitting room,' she said briskly. 'I'll make some coffee and we can listen to some music.'

She began clearing the table.

Jason moved towards her. 'Let me help.'

'I'll do this. Could you see if you can resurrect the fire in the sitting room? I made it when I first came in but it's probably died by now. There are some more logs and firelighters in the basket beside the fire.'

He was leaning over the fireplace when she carried the coffee tray into the tiny sitting room. Billowing smoke surrounded him as he turned round to smile at her.

'I think some of the logs were still damp but I've coaxed them into submission.'

'Good!' she set the tray down on the small table beside the old, squashy, flower-printed sofa. 'It feels beautifully warm already.'

He gave a theatrical cough and a splutter. 'If a little smoky!'

She laughed as she sank down onto the sofa and leaned back against the cushions. 'The fire's always like this for the first few hours. It usually settles down when it's time to go to bed.'

'Then we'll have to stay up all night,' he said, as he accepted the mug of coffee she put into his hands.

Nicky avoided his eyes. Whatever happened tonight, she didn't want to lose herself again in a flurry of passion. She needed to take stock. She had to sort out the troubled emotions that were tumbling around inside her. On the one hand she felt this deep attraction towards Jason, but on the other she needed to remain detached from real emotion if she were to teach him a lesson. But doubts about Sue were lurking in the dark recesses of her mind. She could quell them temporarily, but until she knew the full truth it would be difficult to conduct a feud against Jason.

She put on one of her favourite CDs, Mendelssohn's violin concerto. Leaning against the back of the sofa, Nicky kept very still when Jason's arm drew her against him. Little by little she could feel herself relaxing completely. Her eyelids felt so heavy. She closed her eyes. The music swam over her, soothing her troubled spirits. Jason's arm around her was so comforting...

Nicky awoke with a start. Where was she? The fire had gone out and Jason was fast asleep beside her, his head against a cushion, his arm still loosely around her shoulders. She glanced at the clock. It was way past midnight. Gently she got up and switched off the CD player. As she moved, Jason woke up and stared around him, his eyes blinking as he took in the unfamiliar surroundings.

He gave a long, slow, languid smile. 'Come here,' he whispered huskily.

Nicky pretended not to hear as she raked the ashes to the sides of the fire grate, without turning round. She needed time to think.

He was already standing when she turned, obviously having taken the hint. Again, she glimpsed that hurt expression in his eyes. It was an obvious rejection on her part, but she didn't feel able to deal with her complicated emotions that evening.

'Time I wasn't here,' he said briskly.

She followed him to the door. He bent down and brushed his lips against her cheek.

'Thank you for supper.'

'My pleasure.'

She leaned against the door as she watched him zooming off down the deserted street. The neighbours would never believe they'd simply fallen asleep on the sofa! She closed the door behind her.

Returning to the sitting room, she dialled Sue's number in Australia. It would be around lunchtime there and hopefully Sue would be around to answer the phone. Nicky breathed a sigh of relief as she heard her friend's voice.

'Nicky! Two phone calls in the space of—'

'Let's make it quick, Sue. I need some answers. Jason came round for supper this evening and told me some strange story you'd invented about my mother. She was supposed to have been some downtrodden female who'd advised me never to get married because—'

'Nicky, I'm sorry. I'd had a lot to drink and—'

'But why, Sue?' Nicky was trying to remain calm but it was difficult.

'I can't remember,' she said after a long pause.

Nicky's exasperation was mounting. 'Well, I got to thinking that if you could lie about one thing to Jason, maybe you haven't been completely truthful about everything you told me about him. And I'm warning you, Sue. If I go through with this plan only to find out I've been wrong about him...'

'OK, OK, I'll tell you. It was someone else. Jason wasn't the man who made me pregnant.'

Nicky swallowed hard. Sue had begun to sob. Nicky was used to Sue's melodramatic outbursts but this declaration left her stunned. After all they'd been through together, to realise that her friend had been lying all the time, that all the venom Nicky had felt towards Jason had been totally misplaced...

'Sue, who was the man who—?'

'I don't want to talk about it.' The sobs had vanished and Sue was ominously calm now. Nicky could barely recognise her voice. 'I had my reasons for saying it was Jason.'

'But it was a terrible lie, Sue! To blacken Jason's character like you did and—'

'I think we should make a deal,' Sue broke in, her voice flat and devoid of emotion. 'You've been lying to Jason by pretending you wanted an affair with him. If he finds out, he'll never trust you again. Well, I won't contact him and tell him about that if you don't tell him I lied about him being the father of the baby I had terminated. Agreed?'

'Sue, I was doing it for you so that—'

'You're not to tell Jason I'd said he was the father. He wouldn't be at all pleased if I phoned him and said you'd simply set him up for a fall.'

Nicky's emotions were now as cold as ice. She felt betrayed by this so-called friend. After everything she'd done for her, it came as a terrific shock to find out she was a calculating liar. But from the sound of Sue's voice, it seemed as if she was heading for a nervous breakdown. The termination of the pregnancy and the ensuing months of misery had been traumatic for her.

'I won't tell Jason,' Nicky said quietly.

'Then we've got a deal. I've got to go. Mum's due back any minute. Nicky...'

'Yes?' Nicky noted the pathos that had crept into Sue's voice, the whine that meant she needed something.

'I'm sorry to drop you in it like this, but I've been so ill and I'm in a terrible state. I'm all mixed up. You do understand, don't you?'

Nicky didn't, but she was a doctor and her years of training were standing her in good stead.

'I think you need medical help, Sue,' she said firmly. 'Have you got a good doctor?'

'I can't talk to him. He's a friend of the family and I don't want anyone to know.'

'But you ought to—'

'Mum's coming... Bye!'

CHAPTER FOUR

DRIVING along the mist-shrouded lanes, Nicky was taking no chances. She'd slowed her speed right down to a crawl when she'd found herself going round a hairpin bend that, hopefully, would straighten out soon. The climb from the valley had seemed endless. She peered through the windscreen at the small amount of road revealed by her fog lights. If the mist got any thicker she would have to pull over to the side of the road and wait for it to clear.

She frowned. That might prove hazardous if she were to simply wait at the side of this narrow road. She'd be a sitting duck for any vehicle coming down from the moors. She reflected that she'd longed for a change from negotiating the busy streets of London around her inner city practice, but she hadn't bargained for this!

'Oh, my God!'

Nicky pulled up sharply as what appeared to be a monster from outer space stared at her in the dazzling headlights. It was only a sheep! She chided herself for being so nervous. The sheep gave her a withering look, bleating plaintively before shuffling away into the mist. In her fright, she'd stalled the engine, but thankfully it spluttered to life again and she continued the relentless climb.

And then, miraculously, the mist cleared as she came to the top of the hill and began driving along a wild stretch of moorland. Above her there was even a sun, reluctantly shining through the remaining wisps of mist that lingered over the winter brown heather. It was only November, but winter had definitely arrived with a vengeance in this cold, upland territory.

She glanced at the instructions she'd scribbled on her notepad. The woman on the phone had sounded extremely worried but, from the symptoms she'd described, it didn't seem as if there was anything seriously wrong with her baby. But Nicky had learned over years of general practice to trust every mother's instinct. The mothers were the people who spent twenty-four hours a day observing their children and if they sensed that something wasn't right, it was up to her to take them very seriously.

According to the map she'd consulted, she had another couple of miles to go before she would turn off down the track that led to the woman's house... What was her name? Elaine Bradbury, and the baby was six-month-old Carl.

The road was straight now, the mist completely non-existent. Nicky relaxed and inevitably her thoughts turned to Jason. Sue's revelation that Jason wasn't responsible for the traumatic events that had spoiled her life had changed everything for Nicky. On the one hand she felt enormous relief that she was free to enjoy the feelings of attraction she had for Jason, but on the other she felt a terrible sense of guilt at the way she'd set him up. The start of their relationship at Highdale had been nothing but a sham.

She couldn't bear to think about how Jason would feel if he were to discover the truth about her initial plan to set him up for a fall. And considering Sue's obvious state of instability, it was highly likely that she might renege on their agreement to keep quiet about it. Wouldn't it be better to come clean, tell Jason herself about her initial plan and hope that they could start afresh?

The more she thought about it, the more the situation worried her. She had a good idea how Jason would react to the revelation, and it wasn't promising! But until she told him the truth and faced his reaction, she would have to live with the guilt of what she'd planned to do to him.

Since that evening at her house last month, there had been a certain feeling of strain between them when they'd met at the practice. She sensed that Jason, like herself, was mulling over their relationship which had started so well on that first evening at the dinner party, then had broken off for over a year, only to restart with what had seemed like a whirlwind, spur-of-the-moment romance.

Whenever she allowed herself to think about that heady evening in Jason's flat she knew she wanted to be with him again, even though she was riddled with the guilt of how she'd planned to set him up.

Nicky deliberately hadn't arranged to see him again in an attempt to sort out her confused feelings. They were merely professional colleagues once more. But sometimes she caught him looking at her with an enigmatic expression that she would have loved to have understood. Was he waiting for her to make the first move back to a warmer, more intimate relationship?

She knew Jason had phoned Australia and spoken to Sue's mother because Mrs Gardiner had told her when Nicky had made a further phone call a few days later. Nicky had been alarmed to hear that Sue had flown off to Thailand on a backpacking expedition. Jason would have discovered, as she had, that Mrs Gardiner claimed to have no idea of Sue's itinerary and she maintained that there was no way of contacting Sue until she returned to Australia at some unknown date.

Nicky slowed down the car. This looked like the track that Elaine Bradbury had described on the phone. Yes, there was the dark-stoned house with the ancient oak tree in front of it. Terribly remote! No wonder the poor woman got worried if she had a sick child.

She was welcomed effusively into the pleasantly furnished house by the pretty, dark-haired young mother. The decor and fittings in the house were expensive and in good taste but the house didn't seem like a home. It was more like a show house from a glossy magazine advertisement, still waiting for the people to move in. As Nicky walked along the highly polished wooden floor that led from the front door, she was aware of the intense silence.

'Is Carl your only child?' she asked.

The quietly spoken woman nodded as she opened a door leading into the kitchen. 'Yes, Carl is my first child. We hoped to have more before he was born but now I'm not sure I could take all the worry of another.'

Nicky walked across to the lace-trimmed crib beside the wide open fireplace. This six-month-old baby was very small for his age.

'Was Carl a premature baby?' she asked gently, as she pulled back the covers from the tiny infant.

The mother's brown furrowed. 'Yes. I had a difficult time during the pregnancy. He was born a month early.'

Elaine Bradbury hovered anxiously over Nicky as she undressed the little boy and checked every part of him. It was the unexplained bruise-like mark at the base of his spine that worried Nicky the most. And she didn't like the pallor she discovered when she looked under his eyelids.

She looked down at the tiny baby, lying so peacefully on her lap as she sat in the armchair in front of the fire. He looked like the model of a perfect, peaceful baby. He was such a dear little boy. She could understand why his mother loved him to bits, but also why she was quite rightly worried about him.

'How long has Carl been as lethargic as this, Elaine?'

'Well, he's always been a placid child ever since he was born. My husband, Freddy, says I should be pleased he's such a good baby and sleeps all the time. He says I worry too much because I've got too much time on my hands. But I don't think it's natural for a baby to be so still and quiet. And he's very pale, even though I put him out in the garden in his pram during the summer.'

The young mother was clearly fighting back the tears. Nicky patted her hand gently. 'Is your husband out during the day?'

Elaine blew her nose on a tissue. 'Freddy's an airline pilot and he's away a lot, so I spend all my time with Carl. We moved out here from Leeds soon after he was born. Freddy thought it would be good to bring up our child in the countryside but it's very lonely and…' She dabbed another tissue over her eyes. 'I expect you're going to say I'm an over anxious mother but—'

'No, I'm not.' Nicky squeezed Elaine's hand. 'I'm as concerned as you are and you did quite right to phone the surgery today. Have you taken Carl to the baby clinic recently?'

Elaine's expression became wary. 'I've just never got around to it. I should have signed on at the surgery when I left Leeds but…you see, I don't drive and Freddy said, with such a good baby, it wasn't necessary to take Carl to see a doctor until he was ill.'

'It's always a good idea to keep in touch with the medical services,' Nicky said gently. 'I'm glad you called me out today. I'm concerned about this bruise at the base of Carl's spine.'

'That's what I can't understand,' Elaine said quickly. 'It's always been there. It showed up faintly when he was born and Freddy says it's a birth mark. But it's much more marked now. I haven't had Carl out of my sight so he can't have hurt himself.'

'It looks as if there's some blood collecting under the

skin so I think Carl may have some internal bleeding,' Nicky said gently.

There was no doubt in her mind from her thorough examination of the baby that he was very anaemic. She had met one similar case during her first year as a GP and she knew that swift action was necessary or the child would die.

'But where is the bleeding?' The mother looked distraught.

'That's what we need to find out, and I'm afraid that will mean going to hospital. I'll just have to make a call to Moortown General...'

Fortunately, the paediatric department agreed with Nicky that Carl needed to be admitted immediately. If there was internal bleeding then it was likely that the young patient would need immediate treatment.

Elaine Bradbury proved herself to be a sensible mother when she grasped the fact that hospitalisation was necessary. Nicky drove mother and baby to Moortown General, because she knew that would be much quicker than calling out the ambulance.

The paediatric staff took over from her as soon as she reached the hospital. After a brief discussion with them about her initial diagnosis of anaemia caused by internal bleeding, she left baby Carl and his mother in their capable hands, having been assured that tests and treatment would start immediately.

Driving back up the road to Highdale Practice, she was relieved to find that the low-lying mist had completely cleared. The river in Highdale village, as she'd passed through, had been covered in a thick blanket of steam, rising up to the overhanging branches. But here at Highdale Practice the sun had broken through and the day was positively spring-like.

Apart from the temperature! She shivered as she got out of her heated car.

'Just the girl I'm looking for!'

She looked up at the welcome sound of Jason's voice. He was standing by the open door of the surgery, his hands wrapped around a mug of coffee. The waiting room was empty but Lucy, their receptionist, was working on some letters beside the main desk.

Nicky smiled at Jason as she hurried inside. 'What can I do for you, Doctor?'

This was as far as they got these days, exchanging small talk in the surgery and the occasional discussion about a patient. She looked up at him, noting that he was looking extremely pleased with himself.

'You'll be relieved to hear that I've just had a call from James Beecham.'

'You mean the famous obstetrician, your old friend from medical school days?'

'Not so much of the "old"!'

'Would you like a coffee, Nicky?' Lucy looked up from the letter she was tapping away at her word processor.

'Yes, please. It's been a long, dry morning.' She looked enquiringly at Jason. 'So what did James Beecham say? I presume this is about Belinda Turner, our multiple miscarriage patient.'

She smiled at Lucy and thanked her for the coffee before taking a sip.

'Bring your coffee through to my room,' Jason said in a matter-of-fact tone. 'Take the weight off your legs while we discuss Belinda Turner.'

She followed him into his consulting room, feeling relieved as she sank down on the chair he held out for her.

'Ah! That's better! I've been to the hospital to deliver a

patient and his mother. I was afraid the ambulance service would be delayed because of the awful mist we had earlier.'

'I know. Lucy relayed your message.' Jason's tone was still ultra-professional. 'Richard was about to ask you to do another house call so he had to do it himself.'

'Oh, dear! He won't be pleased.'

He raised an eyebrow. 'It's not your fault. If you think a patient needs emergency admission to hospital then you don't hang around waiting for an ambulance. I'd have done the same. What was the problem?'

'The problem is Carl, a six-month-old baby showing obvious signs of anaemia, possibly caused by internal bleeding. He's got a strange mark at the base of his spine, which looks as if it's got a mass of blood underneath it and—'

'Is young Carl very lethargic, sleeps all day and he's small for his age?' Jason showed his intense interest by the way he interrupted.

'Have you met a case like this before?'

He nodded. 'Only once, during my training when I was planning on specialising in babies. The obstetrics and paediatric firms used to let James and me spend a lot of time on the wards. If my diagnosis is correct, the baby could be suffering from a very rare blood disorder called DBA, which is short for Diamond-Black-fan anaemia. DBA is a result of the bone marrow failing to produce enough red blood cells to carry oxygen around the body.'

Nicky leaned back against the chair as she thought carefully about the implications. 'That sounds like the symptoms experienced by a young patient I had when I was starting out in general practice. I referred him immediately to a paediatric specialist and was told he had to have blood transfusions. I remember the specialist was unable to put a firm diagnosis on the case but the transfusions saved my patient's life.'

Jason nodded gravely. 'That patient of yours may have been suffering from DBA. It's extremely rare and often goes undiagnosed. But when you mentioned that strange bruise-like mark at the base of the baby's spine that gave me a clue. It's actually an ordinary birth mark but because Carl's haemoglobin level has been so low, the birthmark, which in a normal baby wouldn't show up, has become more and more distinguishable the paler the baby has become. This type of birthmark is called a Mongolian blue spot.'

She could see how fired up Jason was.

'You certainly know your stuff about babies,' she said quietly. 'It's such a pity you couldn't pursue your obvious interest and become a specialist like James. Why didn't you?'

He swallowed hard. 'There were family problems at the time.'

'I remember hearing you say that before, but surely you could have gone back to...'

He spread his hands wide. 'It was too late then. Anyway, I find general practice very fulfilling. I'd like to follow up this possible case of DBA. I'll phone the hospital and see what tests and treatment they've come up with.'

Jason began scribbling on a piece of paper. 'His name is Carl...?'

'Bradbury.' She put down her coffee cup. 'I'd be very relieved if you would follow up the case. He's a dear little baby and I feel terribly sorry for the poor mother. She's a shy, timid soul, very much under her husband's thumb from what I can gather.'

He put down his pen and smiled across at her. 'That would never happen to you, Nicky, would it?'

She smiled back, but underneath her calm exterior her heart was racing. She recognised that his subtle, softer voice, with its almost sexy undertones, was the first step towards thawing out the impersonal relationship they'd adopted since that night when she'd cooked him supper, and she knew she was in grave danger of falling in love with him when he spoke to her like that.

'Why do you say that?' she asked.

'Because you're a very independent girl. You don't need a man in your life to look after you.'

'Of course I don't need anyone to look after me,' Nicky said quickly. 'I mean, that's a very outmoded idea. Some women cling to their men, others...'

Nicky drew in her breath in exasperation as she searched for the right words but he leaned forward and touched her lips, oh, so gently with one finger. It was a finger that smelt of the indefinable fragrance she'd experienced when she'd soaped herself in his shower cubicle. She remained absolutely still as deep inside her she felt the turbulence of her senses churning into a maelstrom of intense longing.

He moved his finger from her lips to the side of her cheek but she remained still and silent, not wanting to change the delicious rapport that was building up between them. She knew she simply didn't have the power to break the magic spell that was threatening to overwhelm her.

'I wouldn't have you any other way,' he whispered. 'Don't change.' He leaned nearer. 'I couldn't bear it if you turned out to be just like—'

He broke off, turning away as he stood up and began pacing the room.

'Just like who, Jason?' she asked gently.

'Just like someone I used to know,' he said, so quietly she could barely hear his voice above the humming of the computer sitting on his desk.

He moved back to his desk, squaring his shoulders as if

coming to a decision. 'But I don't want to talk about all that. One day maybe, but not now.'

He stopped, breathing deeply to regain his composure. 'But I asked you in to give you a progress report on Belinda Turner.'

His voice was confident and professional again. 'I've spoken to James this morning and he tells me that Belinda's been admitted to Nightingale, the obstetrics ward at Moortown General. She's in the antenatal section and James has already inserted a Shirodkar suture in her cervix.'

'So he agreed with your diagnosis?'

'Yes. He's stitched up the neck of the womb and it will remain stitched up until she goes into labour. She doesn't seem to mind being kept in hospital until the birth.'

Nicky nodded. 'Belinda told me she would be relieved to be medically supervised for the last few weeks.'

There was a tap on the door then Richard came in. 'Lucy said you were in here with Jason, Nicky. Everything OK with the patient you took to hospital?'

Nicky filled him in on the details of the case and their initial diagnosis.

'They've started on the tests already,' she finished off. 'I'll write up a report as soon as I can. I hope you didn't mind having to cover for me here.'

Richard smiled. 'Not at all. Jane and I pride ourselves in running a caring practice here at Highdale.'

'How is Jane?' Nicky asked.

Richard pulled a wry face. 'Getting more frustrated by the minute, having to rest at home. She's never been incarcerated before. She knows how important it is to rest when you've got placenta praevia but it doesn't make things any easier for her. I know she'd love to see you at Fellside whenever you can spare the time.'

Nicky smiled. 'I'd love to see Jane so I'll certainly make the time at the earliest opportunity.'

'You, too, Jason. The more the merrier.' Richard leaned against Jason's desk. 'Jane hates being a patient. And she misses her father. Robert Crowther was the senior partner at the practice before his cardiac problems forced him to retire. He came to live with us but sadly he died during the summer. He was a real character and we all miss him very much.'

Richard moved towards the door. 'Well, I'll leave you to your discussion. It's good to see new colleagues getting on so well with each other.'

Nicky looked across at Jason as the door closed. 'What do you think Richard meant by that?'

Jason grinned. 'Exactly what he said, that we're getting on well. We are, aren't we?'

She gave him a wary smile. If he only knew what her original intention had been! 'With one or two minor hiccoughs.'

He moved round the desk and pulled her gently to her feet. 'Nothing that can't be ironed out,' he said, before taking her gently into his arms.

She relaxed against him as he kissed her. It felt so good to be back in the circle of his arms again. And now that she knew his character was unblemished she was free to enjoy their relationship. Just so long as she could banish the pangs of guilt she felt when she remembered her initial plan...or confess at the earliest opportunity.

With a determined effort she tried not to think about it. She'd missed Jason so much, but this was neither the time nor the place to show him just how much. Pulling herself away, she still remained close, looking up into his eyes.

'We didn't resolve our differences the last time we were

together,' she said softly. 'I know we needed time to think things over but—'

'It was an unsatisfactory ending to what could have been a perfect evening,' he said slowly.

'Come to supper again,' she said impulsively. 'One day next week.'

That would give her time to make another phone call to Sue's mother. She'd hoped to be able to speak to Sue when she'd phoned and had been rather taken aback when only her parents had been available. She hadn't asked half the questions she wanted to. But she knew, at the same time, she would have to be very discreet.

Had Sue really not told her mother about her termination of the pregnancy? If she hadn't, Nicky would respect her reasons, but she had to find out why Sue had gone so far as to involve Jason in her lies. It wasn't going to be easy getting at the truth unless she could actually speak to the girl.

'No, you come to my flat.' Jason's firm voice broke into her thoughts. 'It's my turn to cook this time. Are you free this evening?'

She hesitated. 'Not until after evening surgery and—'

'That's fine! You'll only have to walk across the courtyard from the surgery and up the rickety old steps. Whenever you can make it. I'll be there all evening.'

He bent his head and kissed her lightly on the lips. Again, she pulled herself away as the sound of her phone ringing in the adjacent room interrupted them. She could have left it to the answering machine but now was a good time to call a deliberate halt before she got carried away.

Jason pushed back his hair from his forehead with one hand, holding the door open with the other. A delicious smell of cooking was coming from inside the kitchen.

Nicky stood at the top of the stone stairs, waiting for him to move back so she could go inside. But first he leaned forward and gave her a long slow kiss on the lips.

Straight from evening surgery, her senses reeled with the surge of emotion his kiss produced. So it was going to be that kind of evening from the start! She knew she wanted an evening of pure pleasure with this exciting man and she couldn't help wishing she'd had time to change into something more seductive. Somehow her severe, tailored, grey suit didn't quite fit the image.

'I feel a bit overdressed,' she said as she stepped inside the kitchen. Jason's hand was still, unnervingly, in the small of her back.

His eyes twinkled. 'There's a whole wardrobe full of Maria's voluminous clothes if you want to slip into something more comfortable.'

She laughed. 'I think I'll pass on that one. I don't think that dress I wore to Patricia's supper party was exactly me.'

'You looked lovely.'

He uncorked a bottle of wine and handed her a glass, motioning her to sit near the fire. She leaned back in the ancient rocking chair that gently rocked every time she moved and took a sip of wine.

'I didn't feel lovely. And how would you know? You were right down at the bottom end of the table and you never gave me a glance.'

'Oh, but I did...when you weren't looking.'

To her annoyance, she could feel a flush spreading over her cheeks as she recognised that they were actually flirting with each other again.

'I phoned Sue's mother in Australia.'

Jason's voice broke into her thoughts. His eyes, looking at her across the short divide of the fireplace were intensely disturbing. A sudden pang of guilt nudged her. She really ought to come clean before she became any more involved, but the thought of breaking up their rapport at this moment was too daunting.

'I know. Mrs Gardiner told me when I phoned,' Nicky said quietly.

'I wanted to ask Sue why she'd told me such a weird story about your mother but she wasn't there. Apparently, she's flown off to Thailand on holiday, on the spur of the moment. She always was an impulsive girl, but her mother didn't seem too happy about it.'

'I can't understand why Sue doesn't want to be contacted on her backpacking trip,' Nicky said quickly. 'It's always possible to leave an address where you can call to pick up your mail, and telephone communications are easy nowadays. Sue was in a low state of health when she went out to stay with her mother. She needed all the support she could get so why she should want to take off on her own like that I—'

'But she's not on her own. Catherine—that's Sue's mother, Mrs Gardiner—told me she's gone off with her boyfriend.'

'Well, that's a relief! I thought she was trekking around by herself and meeting all sorts of undesirables who might take advantage of her.'

Jason leaned across and topped up her wineglass. She'd meant to demur but decided she could always call out the local taxi at the end of the evening. Her car would be safe in the surgery car park until tomorrow. It was so cosy and peaceful sitting here in front of the fire with Jason. She wanted to relax completely and let her hair down.

'I can see you're concerned about Sue,' he said gently.

She hesitated. 'Sue has that effect on people, I think. It's the little-girl-lost syndrome. People fall over themselves to help her.'

'You've got that part of her character exactly right,' he said slowly. 'Sue never grew up. She's the same now as when she was a small child. I think her acting career was a way of escaping from the adult world. She always used to dress up when she was a child and insist that whoever was around became part of an audience. But I think the reality of making a living from the profession wasn't what she thought it would be.'

Nicky nodded in agreement. 'You're so right. I know she was always having to phone home to ask for more funds.'

He was leaping to his feet. 'Oh, dear, do you smell what I smell? Burned carrots!'

He pulled the pan off the cooker. 'Never mind, I've still got some broccoli. I thought the carrots would take longer…' He gave a sheepish laugh. 'As you can see, I'm not much of a cook.'

Nicky put down her glass on the hearth. 'Would you like me to help?'

'No, the instant meal for two is already in the oven. And I remembered to remove the packaging like it said. That's got another five minutes to go…I've just time to cook the broccoli…'

She sat with him at the end of the small kitchen table when the meal was ready. Jason had lit three candles in an ancient candelabra and placed it in the middle of the table.

'One-upmanship, having three candles,' she said as she picked up her fork. 'I only gave you one.'

He laughed. 'But you'd done some real cooking whereas I only had to follow the instructions.'

'This shepherd's pie is delicious.'

'Well done, Highdale village shop!'

'And thanks for the music.' She paused as she chewed on a piece of broccoli, reflecting how thoughtful it was to have put on Mendelssohn's violin concerto, the music they had listened to at her house last month. 'As I recall, we fell asleep during the middle movement...at least, I did.'

He smiled and reached across the table to cover her hand with his own. 'I knew you'd want to hear the whole of the concerto right to the end. This is the same recording, by Yehudi Menuhin. We've both listened to it lots of times, I expect, but it never ceases to thrill me when it reaches that stunning climax.'

The touch of his fingers was taking away her desire for food and making her think of that other voracious, sensual appetite, deep down inside her, which was trying to make itself felt now that she was alone once more with Jason.

He removed his hand and she breathed more easily.

'Nicky, we'll have to make time to go over to one of the symphony concerts in Leeds one evening when we can both escape together.'.

'I'd like that very much.'

There was a warm glow spreading through her as she contemplated their deeply companiable relationship. She was finding they had so much in common. Even without the obvious physical attraction, she found herself wanting to spend as much time with him as she possibly could.

'More shepherd's pie?' He was holding out the dish.

'No, thank you.' She took another mouthful from her plate before conceding defeat and leaning back against her chair.

Jason had dimmed the lights in the kitchen. Only the romantic glow of the candles illuminated the table.

'We'll have our coffee by the fire.' He was standing up, moving plates and dishes from the table and placing them in the sink. 'The advantage of a small flat is that you don't have to walk very far, but I'll have to get started on the property ladder soon. Prices in this area are shooting up all the time.'

'That's why I'm still renting. Patricia and Adam are only charging me a small rent for my little house and I couldn't possibly afford to buy, although it would make economic sense if I could scrape together a deposit. Anyway, for the moment, I'm happy in my little village house. It's got a nice feel to it.'

'Like this place. Lots of happy memories here too, I expect. Richard lived here before he bought Fellside and married Jane. If only these walls could speak!'

Nicky laughed. 'That wouldn't be a good idea.'

The chair rocked gently as she watched him from the fireside, pouring out coffee from the cafetière into a couple of mugs. The intense feeling of physical longing was overwhelming now. She was intensely relieved that the mystery surrounding Jason had been resolved. Could she honestly have believed that he was capable of treating Sue so badly?

Rocking gently in the rosy glow from the fire, mellowed by a couple of glasses of wine, looking across at her handsome, sensitive, wonderful companion, she felt she must have been mad to believe Sue! After meeting him only once for a brief time at Sue's dinner party, she could be forgiven for believing her, but it was good to know that her initial feelings of attraction towards Jason had been justified.

'Why are you looking at me like that?'

She saw that he'd placed his coffee mug in the hearth, every muscle in his athletic body seemingly sensing her physical longing as he leaned towards her.

'I was thinking how different you are to the way I imagined you would be,' she said.

He gave her a slow, sensual smile. 'I was thinking exactly the same about you.'

He stood up and moved towards her. She was already

standing, willing him to take her into his arms. When he pulled her against his hard, virile body, she felt the liquid desires that were clamouring inside her rise to the surface, demanding fulfilment.

They both knew where their passionate fireside embrace was leading. She could feel her excitement mounting as she sensed his arousal. This mutual feeling of longing couldn't be ignored.

Slowly, he lifted her from her feet, cradling her against his chest as he moved towards the bedroom door. She nuzzled her head into his neck, savouring that distinctive masculine aroma pervading his body as her senses turned wild with anticipation.

CHAPTER FIVE

JASON lowered Nicky gently onto the bed and lay down beside her. She reached for the buttons of his shirt, longing to feel his skin against hers. His sensitive hands teased her skin as he removed her blouse. She smiled up into his shadowed, emerald green eyes, feeling herself drowning in the intense tenderness of his expression. Unwilling as she was to believe what was happening to her, she knew that this had to be real love, didn't it? This mutual feeling of belonging couldn't be mere physical passion. Although it wasn't at all what she'd initially planned, she was now hopelessly in love.

She made a determined effort to banish all thoughts of her original plan with regard to Jason. Whatever magic spell was weaving its power over her, she wanted to go along with it as long as it would last. His hands, caressing her now naked body, were driving her wild with a passion she'd never known existed. She ran her fingers over his body, wanting to create the heavenly sensations in Jason that he was creating in her. His hard, virile, manhood was demanding fulfilment but he was holding off so that they could linger together over the heavenly experience, anticipating the heady whirlwind that was to come.

When he finally entered her, at the point when she felt she could hold off no longer, she gave a gasp of incredulity. It was as if she'd stopped living and breathing for herself but was entirely dependent on this other wonderful body that had become one with hers. Nothing in her life had ever prepared her for this feeling. And the mounting rhythm of their movements as they strove to give pleasure to each other in that deep primeval urge was almost more than she could bear. She gasped as she felt herself coming to a climax...

Her voice rose in a crescendo as she cried out in a delicious agony of ecstasy. Wave after wave of pure sensual sensation crashed over her until she felt herself falling...falling...falling back into a deep well of satiated, vibrant, liquid contentment...

Jason was leaning over her when she awoke, a heartrending expression in his eyes. Nicky gave herself up to his tender kiss, the kiss of a satisfied lover, satiated with a night of love-making. Because they had spent the whole night in each other's arms. She couldn't remember how many times they'd rested together before reaching out again to renew their love.

It had been love, hadn't it? She didn't want to think it had been merely physical pleasure, although now in the cold half-light of the early morning she knew she had to come down from cloud nine and think realistically.

'I'll make some coffee,' Jason said, moving away in search of his black towelling robe.

Halfway across the room he became entangled in the pile of clothes they'd tossed onto the floor. He laughed as he picked up the crumpled skirt of her suit.

'I don't think you'll be wearing this skirt into surgery this morning, Doctor.'

Nicky laughed with him. Her feelings were still buoyant and uncomplicated. 'I ought to go home and sort myself out.'

'Have some coffee first. There's plenty of time.'

Her thoughts turned inevitably to Sue. How could she possibly have believed that this warm, loving, man could be responsible for the unhappiness Sue had suffered? She'd never actually seen Sue and Jason in any situation that could possibly have been interpreted as a couple of lovers together. In fact, she'd only ever seen them together on the night of the dinner party. So why had Sue put the blame for her agony on Jason?

He put a coffee-mug on the bedside table and climbed in beside her. She propped herself against the pillows and sipped at her coffee. From outside, she heard the barking of a dog, followed by the crowing of a cock at the nearby farm. It wasn't properly light yet but the world was waking up around her and she had to gather her thoughts together and stop drifting along with the flow, idyllic as it had been.

Patients would need her full support and expertise today. She'd had very little sleep but she would cope. She'd had plenty of practice at being awake all night during her early hospital training. So long as she caught up on her sleep with an early night she would be OK.

It was so peaceful, lying back against the pillows, Jason's head almost touching hers but not quite. They were both silent, but the silence was companionable. There was no need for words when they were both lost in their own thoughts. But she would love to know what he was thinking! Was he reviewing the wonderful, out-of-this-world experience they'd shared together, or were his thoughts totally mundane like hers were becoming as she drifted down from her cloud?

Nicky put down her mug and snuggled against him. He put his arm around her shoulders and held her close.

'What are you thinking?' she whispered.

He hesitated. 'I was actually thinking I owe you an apology for misinterpreting your character.'

Her heart missed a beat. Had he seen through her initial duplicity?

Jason swallowed hard. 'I had expected you might behave as my mother would have done.'

She raised her head to look at him and her heart went out to him as she saw the anguished look in his eyes.

'Your mother?'

He raked his fingers through his hair. 'Sue told me you were the same type as my mother...that was when she made up the story about your own mother having been downtrodden and warning you against marriage. But when you told me that you thought Sue had simply been rambling because she'd had too much to drink at the dinner party, I began to hope that you would be quite different to the picture she'd painted of you.'

She held her breath, her thoughts and emotions in turmoil.

'You see, I've always known it would be impossible for me to form a relationship with someone who behaved as my mother did. My father suffered unbearably because of my mother's fickle behaviour. Everybody who knew us as a family understood what was going on. My mother was the most indiscreet person I've ever known. She simply didn't seem to care what people thought of her.'

He paused, and Nicky could feel his whole body tense as he remembered the sadness and humiliation.

'I remember worrying about my mother's blatant infidelity when I was in my teens. But I realised that, in spite of the hurt it caused, I still loved her because she was my mother...but I could never condone how she behaved. And it had made me resolve that I would find someone I could really trust before I had a relationship with them.'

'You've obviously suffered because of your mother,' she began slowly, wanting to offer some form of comfort but finding the right words difficult to find.

'Not as much as my father did. He loved her in spite of

her infidelity. Watching him suffer as he did, I knew I could never put myself through such agony. I would have to be absolutely sure that if I fell in love with someone I wouldn't be treated in the same way that my mother treated my father.'

She suppressed a shiver as she heard the hard tone in his voice. How could she confess her awful secret now that she knew how he felt? He'd said he'd initially misjudged her character but it was obvious that he trusted her now.

'My father died of a broken heart,' he said quietly. 'I know that's medically impossible and sounds hopelessly melodramatic, but the fact is that after all her affairs and lies my father lost the will to live. He'd forgiven her so many times because he loved her and wanted her back And she always came back until...until she met someone she really fell in love with. Before she finally went away, she told me it was the first time in her life she'd ever been in love.'

'So she never loved your father?'

His eyes took on a fierce expression. 'Never! That's why she was always searching for that special someone...'

'But why did she marry your father?'

He drew in his breath. 'Because I was on the way. When I was about eighteen Mum told me the whole story. Apparently, she was a student nurse at the local hospital near our village in Norfolk. My father was junior partner to my grandfather in our family general practice. They started going out together and she found herself flattered by the attentions of an older, financially stable man. She wasn't taking the relationship seriously and the romance of the situation soon palled. But by this time she'd found she was pregnant. It seemed easier to go along with my father's proposal of marriage than work things out for herself.'

'I suppose she thought she might learn to love your father. It sometimes happens.'

'It certainly didn't happen with my parents. My mother was an orphan, brought up in a children's home, so she had no family background. Just before she left my father, she told me she'd never known real love until she met this latest man…the one she went off with.'

'Was that why you had to return home at the end of your medical training?'

'Yes. My mother phoned me first to tell me she was leaving, and would I keep an eye on my father? I don't know how I was supposed to do that from a hospital in London, but for the first time in my life she sounded as if she cared what happened to him. Maybe this new love had finally mellowed her. Love can do strange things to people.'

He was running a hand through his tousled hair, his expression grim as he relived the awful experiences of the past.

'Anyway, my father phoned soon after that, begging me to come home. He said he couldn't live by himself. He needed me to work with him at the practice because he could feel himself cracking up. I said I would come as soon as I could make arrangements at the hospital. Dad said he would stay at the practice until I'd finished my GP training. There were two fully qualified partners there who supervised my training. As soon as I was fully qualified to take over, Dad retired.'

'It must have been a wrench, leaving the hospital in London.'

He pulled a wry face. 'It was, but I knew my family commitment came first.' He paused. 'Dad had always relied on me for emotional support throughout his difficult times. I knew I couldn't desert him. In the event, my support wasn't strong enough to hold him up. Soon after he retired he took an overdose and it was too late to save him.'

She heard the dreadful fatalistic note in his voice and longed to give him some comfort. Words were inadequate but she had to say something.

'I feel so sorry for you, Jason,' she said gently. 'I simply can't imagine what you must have gone through. But you'd done all you could do, so—'

'I always wonder if I could have done more.' His voice was brisk as he pulled himself up against the pillows. 'I tell myself it's no good worrying about the past...but you can see how I feel about relationships.'

He broke off, his voice cracking under the strain of remembering his past. Then he turned towards her, his eyes veiled.

'That night, at the end of Sue's dinner party, I knew I wanted to see you again. When you didn't turn up for the date we'd agreed on, I decided you must be like my mother, as Sue had warned me. You'd come on strong when we first met, we'd almost made love, and you'd decided you'd had enough of me. That was the way my mother treated her boyfriends. As soon as they were interested in her, she lost interest in them. She enjoyed the novelty of meeting a new man, but she didn't want to pursue a relationship that might necessitate any kind of commitment.'

He took a deep breath and paused, as if searching for the right words. She longed to enlighten him but something deep down inside was telling her to hold back.

'And then, after we met again here at Highdale and we'd almost made love on the day of the storm, I expected you to call a halt to any kind of personal relationship. I thought you would simply ignore me after that and our idyllic time together had been a one-off, never-to-be-repeated experience.'

Nicky touched his cheek, looking up into his soulful eyes

as she remembered how he'd been initially reluctant to accept her supper invitation, saying that she probably wouldn't want to see him again.

'And here we are, having spent an idyllic night together,' she whispered.

'That must prove something, mustn't it?' His voice was husky with renewed passion.

Looking into his sincere, trusting eyes, she wanted to confess, to clear herself of any stumbling blocks between them, but she simply couldn't. She knew she risked losing him if he found out. Jason, this dear vulnerable man whose fickle mother had destroyed his power to trust, would be heartbroken. She hoped fervently that the time would come when she would feel she dared to tell him about what she'd initially planned and maybe he could forgive her. But this wasn't the right moment, when the scars of his suffering because of his mother were so obvious.

Meanwhile, she would continue to hope that Sue would keep her side of the bargain. In any case, she couldn't tell Jason about her own duplicity without revealing how Sue had blackened his name. And she'd promised not to do that.

Nicky opened her eyes as she made a conscious effort to banish her tormenting doubts and fears. Jason had been watching her, his eyes puzzled.

She felt her inward desire rising as he reached for her, but she was trying to remain conscious of the real workaday world they must return to as soon as possible.

'We really ought to—'

His demanding kiss silenced her. She couldn't resist the mounting passion as the sensual currents flooded between them until they became fused in ecstatic union and she was lost once more in the heady maelstrom of their lovemaking...

* * *

Nicky was glad of the excuse to go out on a house call that morning. She felt it would be obvious to the rest of the staff that she and Jason had spent the night together. They would only have to look at the way they avoided each other's eyes and put on an intensely professional manner to cover up their real feelings. In the event, Jason had to go in early to the surgery to take the eight o'clock to nine o'clock appointments so she didn't see him when she checked into the surgery just before nine.

She'd had time to shower at home and put on an entirely different outfit from the one she'd worn yesterday. The ill-fated skirt of the suit which had lain for hours in a crumpled heap on Jason's bedroom floor was now on a hanger, waiting for the next time she got out the steam iron. Today she'd chosen a more casual outfit—a soft woollen, camel-coloured trouser suit with a cream poloneck sweater. The light colours were hardly ideal for her job but it was a warm outfit and wasn't as severe as yesterday's tailored suit.

All the time she'd been dressing she'd been thinking about Jason and wondering if he would approve of how she looked today. Dressing to please your man! Was she on the slippery slope to becoming one of those compliant little women who doted on their men and danced to their tune, whatever the consequences? She hoped not! No, that wouldn't happen to her. She glanced down at the soft muted colours of her trousers. If there were any emergencies requiring her to climb into a crashed lorry today, she was in for trouble!

Thinking about compliant little women made her thoughts turn to Elaine Bradbury, the mother of baby Carl, her anaemic patient. She would check to see if the hospital had rung when she got back from this house call. If they hadn't, she would follow up the case herself because she was anxious to know what progress had been made in diagnosing his condition and what treatment he was having.

Driving round a particularly difficult bend on her descent to the village, she was making a determined effort to be utterly professional. No more daydreaming about Jason even if she did feel as if she'd been off on a different planet for the last few hours. Her patients needed her full concentration.

She'd recognised the name of her next patient as soon as Lucy had passed the message on to her. Harry Marshall was the driver of the lorry that had crashed during the stormy day of young Emma's birthday party at Greystones. He was complaining about his leg injury and had particularly asked for 'that young pretty young lass who looked after me when I crashed my lorry'.

Lucy had given Nicky a winning smile and said she couldn't possibly refuse this house call, could she?

'Harry's quite a character, very well known in the village, and he seems to have taken a shine to you,' Lucy had joked. 'So you'd better be careful.'

Nicky had replied that Lucy needn't worry. Harry had told her he had a wife and six children so she would be well chaperoned!

She reduced speed as she turned into a side street at the top end of the village. She didn't even need the number of the house because Harry's distinctive lorry was parked outside. The crumpled bonnet hadn't yet been replaced but the rest of the lorry looked as if it would be possible to get it on the road again. It was the small car that had suffered the most damage, but fortunately the interior had remained relatively intact so that Megan Bottomley had been able to produce baby Jason in the relative comfort of the back seat. That was another young patient she would like to follow up. The family lived in the area so she made a mental note to find out who was looking after them.

As she parked behind the lorry, a woman with a baby on her hip came out from the house next to Harry's.

'It's time that heap of junk was shifted. It's blocking the light through my kitchen window.'

Harry's door was flung open and the lorry driver, leaning heavily on his crutches, poked his head outside.

'I've told you a thousand times, Doris, I've got nowhere else to park the damn thing. As soon as my leg's better I'll mend it and then I'll be on the road again.'

'And when will that be, Harry Marshall? Christmas? New Year?'

Harry ignored his neighbour's taunts as he smiled at Nicky. 'Come in, Doctor.' He lowered his voice. 'Never mind Doris. She enjoys having something to complain about. Her husband told me in the pub last night that she'd stopped nagging him now that she can go on and on about my lorry.'

Nicky gave him a wry smile. 'So you're fit enough to go to the pub, but not well enough to get yourself to the surgery.'

'Come in, come in,' Harry said, hurriedly ushering her in and pointing to a chair by the fire. 'Park your…park yourself there, Doctor. Now, you see, I can't drive the lorry because I can't change gear, and anyway I need to repair it first. I can't walk up the hill on these crutches. I could catch the bus to the corner of your road but—'

'Don't worry about it, Harry,' she said gently. 'I'm here now so what can I do for you?'

'It's my leg, Doctor. Both of these bones below the knee got broken when I crashed into that little car.' He sank back into a fireside chair and straightened the plaster encased left leg out in front of him.

Nicky knelt down and examined the walking plaster. 'Will you wiggle your toes for me, Harry? That's good, no swelling...'

She leaned back on her heels and looked up at him enquiringly. 'Have you been back to the hospital, to the orthopaedic clinic?'

'Oh, yes. They send the ambulance for me twice a week so I can go to physiotherapy. Then I see the nurse and sometimes the doctor and then they bring me home.'

'Is the leg painful?'

'No.' He paused. 'I mean, yes, it is a bit... Now and then it sort of aches, if you see what I mean.'

Nicky saw exactly what he meant! She moved back to the chair at the other side of the fireplace.

'This isn't about your leg, is it, Harry?' she asked. 'What's really troubling you?'

He cleared his throat. 'I had to wait until the missus was out of the way before I sent for you. She's caught the bus over to Skipton to see her sister—taken the baby with her and the other kids are at school. I wouldn't want her to know how worried I am...'

'Worried about what, Harry?'

'It's this court case. I reckon they're going to send me to prison and I don't know how Annie and the kids will make out without me. They're charging me with dangerous driving. Now, you were there, weren't you, Doctor? You knew what that road was like. You knew what the weather was like. I didn't mean to skid on them leaves, did I?'

Nicky thought very carefully. She had to be careful what she said. As a professional she mustn't prejudge the case. 'I'm sure you didn't mean to skid, Harry. When is the court case?'

'Next week. Moortown Magistrates' Court. I'm absolutely frightened to death about it.'

'Have you got a solicitor?'

Harry shook his head. 'Solicitors cost money and I've got a family to support. While I can't drive my lorry I'm not earning because I work for myself, just ducking and diving, wheeling and dealing, taking a load here and bringing a load back, whatever I can find to make a bit of money. I've always been my own boss ever since I left school and bought my first secondhand lorry with some money me grandad left me,' he finished proudly. 'I've always made a living and put a bit by for a rainy day and never asked for no handouts.'

She recognised the toughness in this salt of the earth man whose main aim in life was to provide for his family.

'You need a solicitor, Harry. Hasn't anybody told you it's possible to have one free? You could get legal aid.'

Harry frowned. 'There was a form to fill in when I got notice of the date they wanted me in court, but it looked like charity to me and I hate filling in forms. Anyway, I don't stand a chance, do I? They've already decided it was my fault. It wasn't that poor woman's fault who was having the baby, was it? I thought I might as well tell them how it all happened and—'

'You do need a solicitor, Harry,' Nicky put in quickly. 'Otherwise…'

Otherwise he wouldn't have a chance if he stood up in court and gave the damning indictment he'd just delivered! She thought quickly of ways round the dilemma.

'I'll phone up and set the wheels in motion for your legal-aid application if you like. It's a standard procedure so you don't need to think you're receiving charity, Harry.'

She couldn't think why she was taking such an interest in this case, but she felt a certain responsibility for this vulnerable, kind-hearted man. She couldn't help remembering how brave and undemanding he'd been as he'd sat in his cab, enduring the pain and asking with great concern about the occupants of the car he'd crashed into.

Harry gave a sigh of relief. 'If that's what you think I should do, Doctor, then I'll go along with you. If you're sure I won't have to pay...'

She stood up. 'I'm sure. I'll get someone to contact you before next week so that you can discuss what's going to happen.'

'There's just one more thing before you go...' Harry looked like a small boy begging the teacher to be kind to him.

Nicky's heart went out to him as she sat down again. 'And what's that, Harry?' she asked gently.

'I haven't been able to sleep since I knew they were taking me to court. I lie awake at night, trying not to waken Annie, and then I'm that tired in the morning... I just wondered if you could give me something, Doctor.'

She hesitated. The policy at Highdale Practice was to avoid giving out sleeping pills except in cases where no alternative treatment could be provided. Harry had another week of worrying before his case came up and she didn't want him to be completely washed out on the actual day.

'I'll give you enough pills to see you through to the day you have to go to court,' she said quietly.

'But what if they put me in prison and—?'

'Let's take one day at a time,' she said quickly. 'Whatever happens, you'll get medical help if you need it.'

Nicky searched in her medical bag for the emergency supply of pills she always carried with her and counted out the required amount into a small packet before standing up.

'Take one of these before you go to bed.'

Harry hobbled to his feet, leaning heavily on his crutches. 'You're very kind, Doctor. Got a heart of gold, you have. I knew you'd sort me out.'

All the way back up the hill she found herself thinking about poor Harry. It would be touch and go how the magistrates viewed the case. The outcome of dangerous driving cases was notoriously difficult to predict. The police would have their findings about the skid marks and other evidence they'd gleaned in the aftermath of the crash.

But she was a doctor, not a lawyer, and she felt herself way out of her depth. She mustn't allow her own biased opinion of her kind-hearted patient to cloud her judgement. If he was proved guilty then that was it... But if she could find the right solicitor...

She stared at the phone after she'd put it down, not even hearing the tapping on her consulting room door. She'd had to wait until the end of the morning to make that important phone call because she'd had a long list of patients to see.

She looked up when she realised that Jason was standing in front of her desk.

He leaned forward, putting his hands on the edge. 'You look miles away. What's the problem?'

She leaned back, forcing herself to smile so that some of her tension would be released.

'It's Harry Marshall. You remember the man who was driving the lorry that crashed on Emma's birthday?'

Jason nodded. 'Is there a problem with his leg?'

She pulled a wry face. 'His leg's fine and he's getting good outpatient treatment at the hospital. As we thought, he'd fractured his tibia and fibula but it's healing nicely. It's the court case looming over him that's making him ill with worry. I've put him on sedatives to see him through the nights. Apparently, he's getting very little sleep so although I would have liked to have tried some other form of treatment I—'

'No need to justify yourself,' Jason said quickly. 'You

understand the case better than anyone else and Harry's hardly likely to become addicted after only a week's course.'

She leaned back against her chair and smiled up at him. 'That's what I thought.' She hesitated. 'I've just been trying to arrange legal aid for him. He hadn't got himself a solicitor and he really needs one. They're going to get back to me tomorrow about that, but I think—'

'And I think you've done enough for one morning, Doctor. Time to switch off. How about a pub lunch with a medical colleague?'

She smiled. Jason's exhilarating attitude was so refreshing. If anyone could take her out of herself it was him.

'Depends who the colleague is.'

'He drives a mean little sports car and he's not averse to frightening vulnerable lady drivers as they drive their old bangers up hills on stormy days.'

'So you *were* trying to frighten me! You rotten…!'

He leaned across the desk and kissed the tip of her nose. 'Not intentionally. But when I saw the anxious way you kept your eyes glued to your rear-view mirror I could see you didn't trust me. That was why I came across in the pouring rain to offer you my parking space to make amends.'

'And I thought you were simply being chivalrous. Come on, I think your pub lunch idea sounds great.'

There was a cosy warmth and a friendly buzz of conversation as they crossed the ancient flagstones in the Coach and Horses. Set high up on the hill above Highdale, it was a favourite watering-hole with people who wanted to escape from the towns that were in striking distance for a congenial lunch. And because it was crowded, Nicky felt that they could remain anonymous.

If there were patients or other colleagues here, nobody would conjecture why she and Jason were on their own. It wouldn't be misconstrued as a romantic assignation even if that was what it felt like at the moment. The memories of their love-making last night were never far away. She only had to look at Jason today to experience a nostalgic tingling feeling running down her spine.

Watching him at the bar now, the top of his dark head almost touching the beer tankards hanging from hooks above the counter, she felt her heart turn over with love. How was this all going to end? She hadn't been ready for the speed with which they'd become lovers.

He was signalling to her from the bar now, pointing to the huge blackboard on the wall. There were several hot dishes chalked in large letters. She mouthed back roast beef, miming a cow's horns with her hands at the side of her head. Having secured a table by the fire, she wasn't going to risk losing it by going over to the bar. She saw Jason laughing at her mime before he turned back to give his order over the bar. Several other people also seemed amused, so she hastily put down her hands.

Jason returned from the bar with their drinks. She'd opted for a glass of wine but Jason was making do with a soft drink because he was driving. He'd already suggested they go to see Jane that afternoon as they were both off duty, so she knew she wouldn't have to drive for a few hours. One glass of wine at this stage wouldn't harm her.

The roast beef came with all the trimmings—Yorkshire pudding, roast potatoes, carrots, peas and lashings of thick gravy.

'Would you like to go for a walk after we've seen Jane?' Jason asked, pausing to spear a piece of Yorkshire pudding onto his fork.

Nicky looked across at the window. The sky had cleared

after a dull morning and the pale November sun was beginning to peep out from behind a cloud.

She smiled. 'I noticed that awful wind had dropped when we got out of the car. It could be a nice afternoon.'

'Is that Nicky-speak for yes?'

'It certainly is. But we won't stay too long at Jane's. It soon gets dark now.'

'Don't worry. It's my turn for evening surgery so we won't hang about. Do you want to stop off and put on some warm clothing?' He was eyeing her light-coloured woollen suit. 'You look absolutely charming, but hardly dressed for muddy paths.'

She looked across the small table. 'Won't it take too long if we have to call in and change at your place and mine?'

He gave her a rakish grin. 'Not if we stick to what we're supposed to be doing and don't get carried away. I've already phoned Jane so she's expecting us as soon as we can make it.'

Nicky knew her cheeks were turning pink at the thought that either of them could even contemplate another session of love-making after the exhausting night they'd spent together.

'I'll take all of five minutes to change,' she said quickly.

He reached across the table and squeezed her hand. 'Spoilsport!'

CHAPTER SIX

THEY'D both stuck to their resolutions at their respective homes and changed with minimum fuss and maximum speed so that they arrived at Fellside early in the afternoon. It was Patricia who opened the door. She said she'd decided on a spur-of-the-moment visit as she often did now that she was only working two mornings a week at the practice.

Jane was delighted to see them. She was lying on the sofa in the large drawing room, propped up against cushions.

'Mrs Bairstow, my housekeeper, insists I put my feet up as much as possible. I honestly think she'd prefer me to stay in bed, but I've seen too many antenatal patients who've had problems because of excessive inactivity. She's been with the family since my mother died when I was quite young, so she mothers me all the time. Little Edward is having his afternoon nap upstairs.'

Nicky saw that Patricia's baby, Matthew, was also fast asleep, strapped into his car seat in the bay window.

'Rebecca and Emma have gone to the kitchen to help Mrs Bairstow make the tea,' Jane said. 'My wonderful housekeeper loves children. She's missing my father, as we all are, and she's only happy when the house is full of children.'

The tea, when it came, was a typical Yorkshire afternoon tea of home-made cakes and biscuits. Mrs Bairstow was in her element as she insisted everybody try the delicacies she'd made that morning, and Nicky was glad that she and Jason had promised themselves a walk at the end of this.

She was still feeling replete after her roast-beef lunch. Patricia's daughters had been given the task of handing round the goodies, so Nicky felt she couldn't refuse them.

'Only a few more weeks and I'll be on my feet again,' Jane said, munching on a piece of carrot cake.

'James Beecham is hoping I'll go to full term, which would be mid-January, and I know that would make sense. But if we get any complications because of the placenta praevia he'll have to induce or possibly do a Caesarean. I'm taking one day at a time, but the way I feel at the moment I'll be glad when it's all over and I'm holding the little mite in my arms.'

Nicky felt a shiver of apprehension. She didn't like the unusual pallor of Jane's face. The strain of the last few weeks since she'd been given the worrying diagnosis was beginning to show.

'The worst thing about being a pregnant doctor is that when you've got something like placenta praevia you realise the danger you're in,' Jane said quietly. 'Sorry, I don't mean to depress you all but—'

'Jane, you're among friends and it's good to express your feelings,' Patricia said quickly. 'As a doctor myself, I can imagine what you're going through.'

'And I feel so helpless, lying here like an old invalid!' Jane said, pulling herself up against the cushions until she was sitting bolt upright. 'I want to be getting on with all the Christmas preparations and—'

'Christmas is weeks away!' Nicky said.

'Not in Yorkshire!' Patricia said with a wry smile. 'We started making our Christmas puddings in January—not me personally, of course.' She gave a self-deprecating laugh. 'But Christmas in Yorkshire is a mind-boggling occasion. There are days and days of feasting, log fires, kisses under the mistletoe, holly hanging from the beams, log fires, presents on the Christmas tree... I'm getting quite carried away at the thought of it but, take it from me, it's out of this world!'

'It sounds wonderful!' Nicky said.

'Lots of preparation involved,' Jane put in wryly. 'Poor Richard won't know what's hit him when I give him our present list!'

'We'll all help,' Jason said. 'I'm a good packhorse. You can send me out for the heavy stuff whenever you like.'

'I think Jane cheered up while we were there, don't you?' Nicky said, as they walked up the uneven, stony, hill path above Fellside.

'I think she put on a good act of looking more cheerful,' Jason replied. 'But she's in good hands. James Beecham is an excellent obstetrician.'

She smiled. 'I believe you've mentioned the fact before once or twice.'

Jason laughed. 'I know you think I'm biased in his favour because he was a mate of mine at medical school but he really is one of the top men in the country.'

'As you would have been if you'd specialised in obstetrics,' she said quietly.

'Believe me, I don't regret going into general practice,' he said firmly. 'Especially when I get such interesting colleagues.'

He turned and put his arm around her shoulders. They were standing on the brow of the hill with a panoramic view of the surrounding countryside. She stood stock still, enjoying the sensual feeling of rapport that being close to Jason induced in her. Far below them, Fellside looked like a little doll's house.

Jason took hold of her hand as they began walking over the brow of the hill and down into what looked like a deserted valley. A stream ran beside the path and a couple of sheep cropped the grass beside it.

'Wouldn't it be wonderful to own a place like Fellside?' she said, feeling guilty at her envious thoughts. 'I've never owned anything more than a secondhand car. One day I'll—'

She stopped dead in her tracks as there, right in front of them, she saw the dearest little cottage. Well, it wasn't exactly small, because she could see several outbuildings sprawling away at the back. But the thing that caught her eye was the huge sign that read, FOR SALE.

She swallowed hard. Already she had a feeling about the place. Nestling in a hollow in the hillside of this different, smaller valley, it would be protected from the fierce winds that raged down the wide Highdale valley. From where she was standing, it looked completely deserted and definitely in need of some repair. Which could mean that it might be going cheap.

'I think I've just seen the cottage I want to buy,' Nicky said slowly, as if in a trance.

'What, that old place down there? You can't be serious! It looks as if the sheep live in it. Half the windows have gone and—'

'I'm going to have a look, anyway.' She was running down the path now, aware that Jason was chasing after her, telling her that she must be mad.

But when they got up close he quietened and had to admit that the place had possibilities.

'You'd have to do a lot of work on it. It looks like it needs a new roof, definitely new windows and—'

'Then I might be able to get it cheap.' She was fired up with enthusiasm as she wrote the telephone number of the estate agent down on a piece of paper and put it into her anorak pocket. 'It's worth a try. I could continue renting my village house until this place was habitable and then move in.'

He raised his eyebrows. 'And how would you get to the practice?'

'There's a track leading away down the hill. Look! It starts at the garden gateway.'

He grinned. 'That's all it is, a track, and a very bumpy one at that.'

She pulled a wry face. 'Well, I haven't got a posh car like yours so it wouldn't matter.' She hesitated as her enthusiasm waned. 'Anyway, it would take ages for me to get the workmen to…and I might not be able to pay what they're asking and I probably couldn't afford the repairs…'

'You're getting cold feet, aren't you?'

'No!' she lied. 'I'm going to go for it. Nothing ventured…'

Jason pulled her down beside him on a wobbly wooden bench inside the rickety stone porch. 'I've got to admit, it certainly has bags of atmosphere. It's beginning to grow on me.'

'Like the ivy.' She pulled off a strand that had strayed down from just above his head.

'Yes, it has possibilities,' he said slowly, looking up at the stone roof of the porch.

'I've always longed to own a house,' Nicky said quietly. 'My parents never got around to buying one until they retired. They were always on the move because my father was in the army.'

'Did you go with them?'

'I flew out to join them about once a year during the long school holiday. Hong Kong, Singapore, India… It was always wonderful to be with my parents but the visits never lasted long enough. In the shorter school holidays I went to stay with my mother's aunt in Devon. She died last year and that was when I started thinking about getting out of London. I hadn't got a country base to go to any more, so I began scouring the ads in medical magazines, looking for a country practice so that…'

She stopped when she saw the look of astonishment on his face.

'That must have been about the same time I started doing exactly the same thing,' Jason said. 'I'd reached the point where I couldn't stand the endless, anonymous streets around the London practice. I was longing to breathe the clean country air again.'

Nicky stared at him. 'Great minds think alike,' she said. 'It's strange we should meet in London at Sue's and then find ourselves working together up here. It's almost as if—'

She broke off in embarrassment, checking her wayward tongue from saying something she would regret. It was much too early in their relationship to speculate that it seemed like destiny that they should be thrown together like this. And there were obstacles to be overcome.

She was rapidly coming to the conclusion that as soon as she could make contact with Sue again she would have to convince her to come clean with Jason and tell him how she'd claimed he'd made her pregnant and abandoned her. That would enable Nicky to explain how, in misplaced loyalty to her friend, she'd made a plan to set Jason up. Jason had a right to know all that, but it was up to Sue to set the ball rolling. Nicky couldn't tell her part in the story without involving Sue, and she wanted to be totally honest with Jason.

Becoming as close as they were, they shouldn't have secrets between each other. When the time came she would have to weather his reaction to the revelations and hope that it wouldn't destroy his trust in her.

'Why did you leave your family practice in Norfolk and

go to London?' she asked quickly, before Jason could sense that she was worrying about something that concerned him.

He gave a resigned sigh. 'There was a big reorganisation of the medical services in the area. Our practice was going to be merged with another practice in the nearby town and we were going to have to work in a new building several miles away. I didn't fancy that at all so I decided to sell up and go back to London to be near the friends and colleagues I'd had before my father asked me to help him in Norfolk.'

He was silent for a few seconds. As Nicky waited she could see from his expression that the move had been a mistake.

'Nothing ever stands still,' he said slowly.

'The London scene had changed and so had I. Many of my old friends had moved away and those who remained were, like me, no longer young, carefree medical students. I discovered I was expected to work long, difficult, anti-social hours at the practice. Soon after I started work, I had an affair with a girl I'd known when we were at medical school together. She moved into my flat for a few months but it didn't work out. We got bored with each other and drifted apart. I'd bought a lovely flat with a view of the Thames, but it never felt like home. I always knew I would find my spiritual home in the country somewhere…and I think I have.'

'Me, too,' she said quietly, as she looked out at the peaceful scene beyond the porch. An inquisitive sheep had wandered up the uneven path and was staring at her. When Nicky raised her head it turned and stumbled away towards the trees at the end of the wild garden.

'So when I got this job I was more than happy to sell my London flat and move north.'

'You must have got a good price if it had a view of the river.'

'I did. I'd been lucky to be able to afford it when I moved there from Norfolk. Prices were shooting up all the time, but I had the money I'd got from selling the family house and practice.'

'I like the way you say "family house",' she reflected, almost to herself. 'I always hoped my parents would buy a house where we could be a real family. But when Dad retired they bought a place in Spain. I go out to see them occasionally but it's not the same. I suppose I'll just have to wait until I've got my own family.'

He turned to look at her, his eyes tender. 'And when will that be?'

'Maybe I'll buy this place and adopt a few sheep,' she quipped, feeling the tension rising between them.

He bent his head and kissed her tenderly on the lips, his arms reaching out to hold her against him. The aftermath of their love-making still lingered even after the hours of work and pleasure which should have diluted the sensual feelings. Nicky wondered if Jason still felt as she did.

She moved gently in his arms, knowing that her body would respond to any suggestion of love-making, but her head was insisting she didn't get carried away.

'It's getting dark. You have to be in surgery soon, Jason.'

His whimsical smile had a rakish element as he looked down at her. 'It's a good thing one of us can remain sensible.'

He stood up and reached down to pull her to her feet. 'Let's go back and collect the car.'

The flames from the sitting-room fire licked round the logs, sending a warm glow across the hearthrug. Curled up on the sofa, Nicky listened to the wind outside. The Mozart piano concerto she'd been listening to had finished and she was simply enjoying the peaceful sounds of the country village outside. Voices of the people walking past her window came through to her occasionally. Some of them sounded as if they'd been to the pub and she enjoyed hearing the laughter and chattering.

It wasn't anything like the raucous outbreaks she'd heard in London, and once more she felt glad that she'd made the move. She would be even happier if she could buy that rustic cottage. There would only be the sound of the sheep to disturb her off-duty times...unless, of course...

She dismissed the idyllic fantasy as soon as it arose. She and Jason sitting beside a log fire, having decided to live together in the cottage.

He hadn't phoned after surgery this evening. She hadn't expected him to...had she? Well, if she was honest with herself, she'd rather hoped he might have just called to say goodnight. But, then, it was no bad thing to try to cool the temperature of their relationship. Especially when she didn't know where the relationship was going and there were still lingering doubts on both sides.

She glanced at the clock. It was almost midnight and she really ought to go and get her beauty sleep, but the temptation to linger by the fire was too much to resist. Besides, it wasn't often she had the opportunity to do absolutely nothing. Her thoughts turned once more to Sue.

She had to try and contact Sue and the timing now would be just right. Maybe, just maybe, Sue's mother might be more helpful than she'd been last time.

'Mrs Gardiner?' It never ceased to amaze her how quickly she could make a connection through to the other side of the world. 'It's Nicky Devlin. I phoned you last month about—'

'Yes, I remember you. And you're in luck. Sue got back

from Thailand yesterday. I haven't got around to telling her you phoned. Would you like to speak to her?'

Would she! She could hardly control her excitement as she waited for Sue's voice to come on the line.

'Nicky! How nice to hear from you.' Sue lowered her voice. 'Hold on a moment... It's OK now. Mum's in the other room. You haven't told Jason about—?'

'I haven't told Jason about anything, but I think you should.' Nicky kept her voice friendly but firm. 'He shouldn't be kept in the dark like this. He deserves more than—'

'Nicky, I can't talk now.' Sue's voice was so quiet she could hardly hear it. 'I'll phone you some time when I can. Don't phone me here. Mum doesn't know about...my operation and everything.'

Nicky heard footsteps in the background before a definite shift to a false, brighter tone. 'Yes, thank you, I really enjoyed Thailand.'

Sue's voice now changed to a chatty impersonal tone, making it obvious to Nicky that Mrs Gardiner was somewhere near.

'I'm coming over to London again soon. I've got a part in a play...well, actually my agent has arranged the audition and it will be lovely to get back into some real work.'

'Ring me again as soon as you can talk,' Nicky said firmly, as she felt her frustration rising again.

'Yes, I'll look forward to that,' the bright, unnatural voice told her before the line went dead.

Slowly, Nicky got up from the sofa and began raking the half-burnt logs to the sides of the grate. The flames had died and only the dying embers remained. A bit like her feelings! She'd been so buoyed up when she'd found she could actually speak to Sue. But her hopes that she might persuade Sue to put Jason in the picture had been dashed within seconds.

Her phone was ringing! Sue was calling back. She threw the poker down on the hearth as she grabbed the phone.

'Sue?'

There was a couple of seconds' silence before she heard, 'No, it's me, Jason. Why did you think it might be Sue?'

Her heart leapt into her mouth. For a moment she couldn't reply. Carefully, she selected her words.

'I made a phone call to Sue just now and we were cut off…well, actually she didn't want to talk…'

Careful! Her tongue was running away with her.

'She didn't want to talk? Why was that?'

Jason sounded so surprised but, then, he would because he was totally ignorant of the events that had led up to Sue going out to Australia to lick her wounds. Nicky wanted so much to enlighten him, but it wasn't her secret to tell.

She took a deep breath. 'I think Sue was tired. She's just got back from Thailand.'

She'd wanted to hear the sound of his voice all evening, but now she needed to be alone with her thoughts to try and sort out what she was going to handle the situation.

'You said her health hadn't been good. Is she simply tired from the journey or tired because she's still run down?'

Jason sounded like the concerned, caring doctor he was. Nicky swallowed hard, consumed with guilt at the secrets she was hiding from him.

'Sue's feeling better than she was. I think the holiday with her boyfriend has helped, but she didn't want to talk about it with her mother hovering in the background.'

'I'm surprised she was allowed to go away with a boyfriend. Catherine's a bit strait-laced and very protective of her beloved daughter. Did you find out who this boyfriend is?'

He sounded extremely interested, but he had known Sue since she was small.

'She didn't want to tell me anything,' she replied evenly.

'I'll give her a call and try to find out why she told me that fictitious story about your background and painted your character in that unflattering way.'

'I don't think that would be a good idea,' she said quickly.

'Why ever not?'

She was taken aback by the cool, impersonal tone he'd suddenly adopted.

'Jason, you can please yourself, of course, but Sue gave me the impression she didn't want to take any more calls in Australia.'

She waited for him to reply. Come on...come on... After what seemed an unbearable length of time, she jumped in, unable to stand the ominous silence.

'Sue told me she was coming to England soon for an audition. She's also going to phone me when she can.'

'Well, that's a bit more hopeful... I'll say goodnight, then. It's been a long day.'

'Yes, hasn't it?'

She realised she was talking to a dead phone. It certainly had been a long day, a day that had started in Jason's arms, snuggled against him after a long night of passionate, ecstatic love-making. And a day that had ended on a sour note as, once again, she'd been unable to be totally honest with him.

Nicky was relieved to be able to immerse herself in her work during the following week because there was a very uneasy feeling of constraint between Jason and herself.

Neither of them actually alluded to the contact Nicky had made with Sue but it was nevertheless always there, holding them apart.

She was extremely busy and she tried to tell herself that when Sue phoned everything could be cleared up, but the thought didn't give her much comfort—or indeed much hope!

Looking out of her consulting-room window, she felt as bleak as the landscape. A thin layer of snow had peppered the tops of the hills during the night even though they hadn't reached the end of November yet. It was bitterly cold outside and she was beginning to wonder if she would be tough enough to cope with a harsh northern winter. A couple of weeks at Christmas in the relatively mild winters of Devon close to the sea in her great-aunt's well-insulated house was the only preparation she'd had for a country winter. And here she would be expected to trek out in every kind of bad weather to see her patients in their remote dwellings.

Had she bitten off more than she could chew? She had as far as Jason was concerned, because she had no idea how to handle the sudden cold spell in their relationship.

And to add to Nicky's sombre mood was the disappointment she'd felt when she'd phoned the estate agent to ask the price of the cottage she'd set her heart on. It was astronomical, considering the state of the place! But as the estate agent had been quick to point out, the cottage had infinite possibilites. Situated in a delightful rural setting, it was much sought after. In fact, they had just received an offer in excess of the asking price.

Some people must have money to burn! That had been her reaction as she'd ended the phone conversation before the estate agent could whet her appetite even further. Well, whoever was thinking of buying it would need to have lots of money to do the place up. If she could have bought the cottage for a fraction of the asking price she would have done the essential repairs and improved it little by little, investing some of her salary each month in the project.

She would have moved in as soon as it was vaguely habitable, built a huge log fire in the evenings and made herself cosily comfortable. But that wasn't going to happen now. It had been her dream castle and now it had vanished and she'd better stop thinking about what might have been.

Her intercom buzzed and she brought her thoughts back to her next patient. She gave a welcoming smile as Elaine Bradbury came in, carrying little Carl in her arms.

'It's nice to see you again, Elaine. Do sit down.'

She waited until the nervous young mother had settled herself in a chair, the baby clutched tightly against her, before she continued.

'I'm glad you've come in. I had a report from the hospital about Carl and I was going to call in and see how he was.'

Elaine smiled. Nicky thought she was looking a little more confident as she laid baby Carl across her lap, unwrapping the warm, woollen blanket that had been wrapped around him.

'I thought I'd save you the trouble, Doctor, and as Freddy has a few days off before he flies again he said he'd run me to the surgery. As you probably know, we were only in hospital for a few days. The medical staff were lovely. They didn't mind that I wanted to stay with Carl and they even gave us a little side ward all to ourselves. I'm so grateful to you for taking us there because one of the doctors told me that Carl would have just slipped into a peaceful sleep and died if he hadn't been treated.'

Nicky swallowed hard. She'd realised how serious Carl's condition was and she couldn't bear to think about what would have happened if she hadn't gone out to see Elaine that day.

'The report from the hospital said that they'd given Carl some blood transfusions to counteract the anaemia,' she said carefully.

'Did they tell you he may have to go back in and have some more?'

Nicky nodded. 'Yes. Carl's in a stable condition at the moment but the specialist, Jonathan Platt, wants to keep an eye on him.'

'Apparently, he's got some rare disease called DBA, which I've never heard of. Do you think you could explain it to me, Dr Devlin, preferably in words of one syllable? I was never very bright at school.'

There was a self-deprecating grin on Elaine's face as she said this, and Nicky gathered that although she could make jokes about being supposedly dim, she was probably much brighter than everybody gave her credit for—her husband included!

'DBA, or Diamond-Black-fan anaemia, results from the bone marrow failing to produce enough red blood cells to carry oxygen round the body. That's why Carl looked so pale before he had the transfusions. He's a much better colour now, isn't he?'

Nicky held out her arms and Elaine put the baby into them. He was still incredibly small for a seven-month-old baby but he was much stronger than the lifeless infant she'd examined a month ago. She took him through to her examination cubicle and laid him out on the couch. He even managed a dear little smile as she tickled his tummy.

'The blood transfusions have made an enormous difference,' Nicky said as she handed Carl back to his mother at the end of the examination. 'The steroids that he's taking will also strengthen him.'

'To be honest, I'm a bit worried about the medication,' Elaine said slowly, holding her precious baby protectively against her. 'I've read such differing opinions about whether or not we should take steroids.'

'If steroid medication is well supervised, as it is in Carl's case, and if it's prescribed as a lifesaving medication, I wouldn't hesitate to go along with it,' Nicky said firmly.

'Your specialist is trying Carl on steroids for a month and then he's going to review the situation. Don't worry, he's a man who's very well up in his field. This is a rare disease we're treating and anything that can ease the condition is worth trying.'

The worried mother's frown disappeared. 'Will you call in to see me when you're out near the house, Doctor? Just a five-minute chat will give me confidence again.'

Nicky smiled. 'Of course I will. And meanwhile, don't worry. Just trust Mr Platt because he really does know what he's doing.'

She looked out of the window again as the door closed on her patient. A minute later, Jason put his head round the door and made her jump. 'Have you any more patients to see?'

'No. Elaine Bradbury has just gone home with baby Carl, our DBA patient.'

She tried to recover her composure as Jason came in, closing the door behind him and moving towards her desk.

'Carl is looking stronger,' she carried on hurriedly, intent on keeping the conversation on a professional level. 'He's had blood transfusions and Jonathan Platt has put him on steroids.'

Jason nodded. 'Yes, I spoke to him on the phone the other day. I've been keeping abreast of the case because it's not often you see a patient with DBA.'

'I would have called you in if I'd thought you wanted

to examine Carl,' Nicky said, 'but I knew you were busy with a patient.'

She didn't know why it seemed so necessary to defend her actions. She'd simply forgotten about Jason's intense interest in the case.

'That's OK. I went in to see Carl while he was still in hospital.'

'Elaine asked me to call in when I was out that way,' she went on. 'Maybe you would like to do one of the visits.'

'It would be better if you came with me,' he said evenly. 'Elaine Bradbury seemed very shy and nervous when I met her in hospital. I think she'd prefer to have you there...in fact, so would I.'

She noticed the softening of his tone as he finished speaking. At the same time she experienced a lift in her spirits.

'In fact...' He hesitated before continuing, 'I don't know what's been happening to us for the last week, but we've got to put an end to this feeling of unease when we're together. It's something to do with your phone call to Sue, isn't it?'

He sank down in a chair on the other side of her desk, his eyes watching her warily.

Her pulses were racing. 'It could be to do with my phone call,' she said carefully.

'Well, anyway, it did seem strange at the time and because I'm an inquisitive bloke I decided not to wait until Sue called you. She can be so unreliable when it comes to keeping promises like making phone calls. So I decided to take matters into my own hands and last night I phoned Australia.'

CHAPTER SEVEN

NICKY waited, her pulses racing. 'And what did Sue say?'

'Sue wasn't there. She's already left for England.'

'So was it a waste of a phone call?'

Jason's eyes flickered. 'Not entirely. Catherine and I had a long chat. I used to be very fond of Sue's mother when I was younger. She mothered me when my own mother was gallivanting around.'

'But I thought you said she was strait-laced. Didn't she disapprove of your mother's behaviour?'

'Oh, absolutely! That was why she took such an interest in my welfare when I was growing up. Catherine and Jack had a large house on the edge of the village, right next door to the church. They used to care for all the waifs and strays and they seemed to include me in this category, even though my father was the village doctor. Every time Mum disappeared for a while, they used to invite Dad and me round for meals. But Sue was always something of a rebel. I think she enjoyed shocking her parents.'

'So, what did you find out from your phone call?'

'Catherine said she was worried about Sue. She'd split up with Mike, her boyfriend, while they were in Thailand and she seemed very upset about that when she arrived back. Mike is someone she knew quite well when she was in London, apparently. Did you ever meet him, Nicky?'

Nicky shook her head, but her mind was buzzing with the implications of this revelation that Sue had had a boyfriend in London.

'I don't remember anyone called Mike. In fact, she never

brought any boyfriends back to the flat when I was there. But, then, I didn't see Sue for the last few weeks before she went away. She'd sold the flat to pay off her debts and get the money to go out to Australia.'

'Yes, Catherine was furious with Sue for selling the flat. She and Jack had bought it for her so that she would have a secure base in London. Apparently, she's spent most of the money already on her trip to Thailand. They had to give her the money for her air ticket to England and some money to tide her over until she starts working.'

'Must have been some backpacking trip!'

'That's what I thought.' He paused. 'Where did you live after Sue sold the flat?'

Nicky pulled a face. 'A poky little bedsit just round the corner from the surgery. Sue got an offer she couldn't refuse from some people keen to move in, so I moved out and took the first place that was available. It was soon after that I came up here for interview and after that I couldn't wait to move up here.'

'And where did Sue live for the last few weeks?'

'Oh, she moved into a hotel. Much too expensive for me.'

He was looking puzzled. 'What I couldn't understand when I met you at Sue's dinner party was how you two came to be sharing a flat together. I mean, you're a most unlikely pair of friends. You a doctor with a highly responsible job and Sue with a very dodgy record of trying to keep her head above water in the acting profession. She spent three years at a drama college and enjoyed the life there, but she didn't seem to get much work after that.'

'Acting is a tough profession,' Nicky said.

Jason smiled. 'Almost as tough as ours, but at least we never run out of work.'

'The reason I moved into Sue's flat was because I needed

somewhere decent to live. As soon as I'd finished medical school and actually started earning, I decided to get out of the awful bedsit I was living in. I scanned the advertisements in the local paper and found this one from Sue about a flatshare. I could afford the rent she was asking and it was infinitely more comfortable than the place I was in.'

'And the two of you got on OK?'

'More or less. Sue wasn't the easiest person to live with. Her moods swung from high to very low depending on whether she was getting any work or not. But I put it all down to her temperament as a budding actress. Sometimes she used to get depressed and start crying and I would have to try and cheer her up.'

'Oh, Sue can turn on the waterworks at the drop of a hat. You should have seen her wringing her hands and screaming for days on end if she couldn't get her own way. She got lots of sympathy, I can tell you, and that was what she's always craved. The more she moaned, the more attention she got.'

He hesitated. 'You'll let me know as soon as you get that phone call, won't you?'

'Of course.'

'Maybe we could both go down to London and see her as soon as we have an address,' Jason said.

Nicky felt her spirits soaring. As soon as she could get the two of them together she would insist that Sue tell Jason the truth.

'I'd like that,' she said quietly.

'We could have a great weekend, check into a hotel, go to the theatre or a concert...'

She smiled. 'Sounds great!'

He stood up and came round to her side of the desk, taking hold of her hands and pulling her to her feet so that he could fold her in his arms. She leaned against his hard chest, revelling in the feeling of being together again. Looking up into his eyes, she could see real tenderness there.

They were still standing together, gazing up into each other's eyes when Lucy opened the door and came in with a pile of case notes.

'Oh... I'm so sorry, Nicky. I thought you'd gone.'

The embarrassed receptionist dumped the notes on the nearest chair and made a hasty retreat.

Nicky's face broke into a grin. 'This will be all round the practice by the end of the day.'

Jason laughed. 'Could have been worse. We might have been kissing...something like this...'

As his lips came down on hers, she felt the full strength of his virile body against hers. For an instant her head told her to move away, but her heart took over as she felt the shivers of anticipation running through her. Nothing short of a complete consummation would erase the memories of a whole week without each other.

But not here in the surgery, of course! Even so, she gave herself up to the excitement of his kiss and the promise of what was to come at the earliest opportunity.

'Are you free tonight?' he asked, his voice huskily teasing as they relaxed their embrace.

'What did you have in mind, Doctor?' she asked, her eyes unashamedly flirting with him.

'I thought we could have an intense medical conference together. Something highly stimulating.'

She laughed. 'We'll have to agree on the agenda.'

'Of course. We can discuss it over dinner. I've made enquiries and found this rather swish country house restaurant not too far away from the conference centre...'

'Sounds great. And where exactly is the conference after the dinner to be held?'

'Just across the courtyard from this consulting room, actually. Miriam, my three-legged personal assistant, will preside over the proceedings and—'

The outside phone on her desk started ringing. Lucy must have already gone home and not switched the practice over to the doctors' answering service, knowing that two doctors were still on the premises. Nicky made a valiant effort to change back into efficient professional mode as she picked up the phone.

'Dr Devlin here... Yes, Harry.'

Her smile broadened as she listened to Harry Marshall's good news. She was aware that Jason was watching her enquiringly and she mouthed that she would fill him in later.

'That's only what you deserve, Harry,' she said eventually, then she put the phone down.

Jason smiled. 'I gather that was Harry Marshall, our lorry driver patient from the crash.'

'It most certainly was and it's good news! He's been acquitted of dangerous driving. Harry's solicitor discovered that a motorcyclist had come off his bike at the same spot about an hour earlier. The motorcyclist had escaped injury and managed to get his bike started again. But some oil had been spilt on the road, making the surface hazardous. In court the solicitor also stressed the fact that the estimated speed of the lorry was lower than would normally be expected, which showed that Harry was aware of the treacherous conditions and had reduced his speed accordingly.'

'He must be so relieved!'

She smiled. 'I'm nearly as relieved as he is! I had a dream the other night where I went to visit him in prison.'

'Which just goes to show that you need to get away from your work for a while. I'll pick you up at eight...'

* * *

As she changed out of her workaday suit, Nicky was still amused by the childish nonsense they'd discussed before leaving her consulting room. Well, they'd both been off duty so could be forgiven for relaxing on the surgery premises. She remembered how she'd laughed at the thought of Miriam presiding over their mythical medical conference.

Their laughter had been just what she'd needed to get rid of the tension that had been building up over that long week since she'd spoken to Sue on the phone. She could see that it had been therapeutic for Jason, too.

And tonight was going to be the tonic they both needed. Now, what was she going to wear…?

An hour later, having had a long soak in the bath, she was still no wiser. It had to be something sexy…but not blatantly so. More subtle than sexy…

She riffled through her wardrobe. The black skirt with the side split, and the low-cut cream blouse that she'd never dared to wear…?

Awful! She stared at herself in the long mirror. This blouse would have to go to one of the charity shops. In the end she settled for the grey trouser suit that made her legs look longer than they were and a pale pink, silk shirt with a frilly bit that peeped out of the top of her jacket.

She needn't have worried because Jason told her she looked wonderful as soon as she opened the door. He was looking at her with the sort of expression that told her she could have worn a sack and he would have found her attractive.

'Are you going to ask me in for a drink?' His voice still held that hint of promise she'd heard earlier in the day.

Nicky gave him a long slow smile. 'Don't you think that might delay the proceedings?'

'Would that matter?' His voice was huskily sexy as he

put one hand on the door plinth and looked down at her with infinite tenderness and undisguised longing.

She knew it was up to her to make the decision. She could ask him in and they could cancel the restaurant and spend the entire night together, just the two of them. Heavenly as the prospect seemed to her, she felt it would be nice to hold off the love-making until after dinner. They could savour the feeling of anticipation, and the inevitable conclusion would be all the more exciting.

'I'm looking forward to seeing this restaurant,' she said quickly.

He gave her a rakish grin as he took her arm and led her out to the car. 'So am I.'

The country house restaurant was a very posh place, judging by the outside. Nicky stared up at the rugged stone façade in admiration.

'It looks inviting enough to be a private house.'

'Apparently, that's what it used to be. Adam recommended it to me when I told him I needed somewhere to take a girl I was trying to impress.'

She smiled. 'Did he have any idea who that might be?'

'Not an inkling!' he said, in an exaggerated tone.

'We're going to be the talk of the practice soon.'

'We're in very good company. As we all know, it was working in the practice that brought Jane and Richard and Patricia and Adam together.'

'Must be something in this clean Yorkshire air,' she said, breathing in deeply before they stepped over the stone threshold.

She felt herself immediately enveloped in a warm ambience of sheer luxury, the sort of attention to detail that was only found in a private home. There was none of the brash attempt to impress which was sometimes found in an establishment of this kind. All the antiques fitted in with the discreet decor and looked as if they were lovingly cherished by a family.

They were welcomed by a charming man who looked as if he was the owner of the house but was probably just a very sensitive manager, who made it clear from the start that nothing would be too much trouble.

The table by the window which Jason had asked for was ready for them. Nicky looked out at the darkened sky beyond the lights of the forecourt. She couldn't make out the landscape but she knew that the mysterious hills were out there somewhere, waiting to be illuminated in the moonlight.

She turned to look across the white cloth of the table at Jason who had been watching her. 'I really love living up here!' she told him softly. 'I'm so thankful I decided to leave London. I had no idea…'

She broke off, trying to unravel his enigmatic expression. There were so many things that still had to be sorted out, but for the moment she was happy just to be with Jason in this warm, hospitable corner of England.

She started her meal with a delicate creamed Jerusalem artichoke soup garnished with croûtons. For her main course she'd chosen lamb fillet in a red wine sauce. Jason was having roast partridge.

He looked at her, his eyes twinkling. 'Beats my ready cooked, heated-in-five-minutes offering. You'll never come and have supper with me again after this.'

'Oh, but I will!'

As she scooped up the delicious sorrel mousse that accompanied the lamb she found herself looking forward to a succession of evenings when they would enjoy each other's company over a simple meal. It was good to be spoiled occasionally like this, but cosy evenings by the fireside together were just as exciting.

It would be if she could feel that she dared look ahead to some kind of future where Jason would figure largely. Once she'd convinced Sue to come clean she could face Jason's reaction to her own revelations. Until that time, she wouldn't know what the future held. But for the moment she would simply enjoy the wonderful rapport that existed between them.

'You're looking terribly solemn. Is there something wrong with the lamb?'

Jason's voice interrupted Nicky's thoughts.

'It's delicious!' she said quickly.

He put down his fork. 'So why the troubled expression?'

She hesitated. 'I was just thinking about Sue, wondering how she's going to feel when she gets back to London...with all its memories.'

He frowned and his eyes took on a veiled expression. 'What memories?'

She hesitated. 'She wasn't very happy before she went to Australia.'

'Well, if she was run down she wouldn't be feeling too good, would she?' He raised one eyebrow. 'Hey, come on, let's forget Sue. There's just the two of us this evening and Sue's welfare is one subject that's definitely off the agenda of our post-dinner conference.'

'Talking of after dinner,' she said carefully, 'would you mind if we conferred back at my place? I've got things to do before I go into the surgery tomorrow and—'

'And you want to wake up in your own bed,' he teased.

She smiled. 'I wasn't going to spell it out but, since you mention it, it had crossed my mind.'

'I'll have to phone Miriam and tell her of the change of plan,' he said solemnly.

Nicky laughed. 'I hope it won't upset her busy schedule.'

The waiter had cleared the plates and brought their desserts. Nicky sank her spoon into a white chocolate caramel, flavoured with Grand Marnier which rendered her speechless for some time.

Jason smiled as he reached across the table to cover her hand with his own. 'No need to ask if you enjoyed that. Would you like coffee?'

She hesitated. 'I could make coffee at home.'

'I'd like that.'

His voice, rich with anticipation of the evening ahead, sent shivers down her spine. He turned her hand over, stroking the palm gently before bringing it to his lips.

'I'll get the bill.'

Nicky lay back amid the frothy suds that were bubbling around them. Jason's feet were curled around her end of the bath but the rest of him was submerged beneath the water. He reached over the side and took the bottle of champagne from her makeshift ice bucket. She would never be able to put flowers in that huge vase again without remembering!

'It's a tight squeeze,' she said, as she held out her glass for a top-up.

He smiled as he leaned forward to kiss the tip of her nose. The foam on their faces rubbed off on each other.

She laughed. 'This bubble bath tickles. I'd no idea it was going to feel like this when I bought it.'

'Did you buy it for this special occasion?'

If she hadn't been encased in foam Jason would have seen the pink flush that had spread over her cheeks as she remembered prowling around the local chemist's shop looking for a sexy foam bath. Amazingly, she'd found what she was looking for, discreetly hidden at the back of the remedies for easing arthritic joints. In small print, this exotically perfumed foam bath declared that it was the perfect addition to a shared bath or Jacuzzi.

'You never cease to amaze me, Nicky,' Jason said, his voice husky with tenderness. 'The champagne cooling in the fridge...'

'Doesn't everyone have champagne in the fridge?' she asked, opening her eyes innocently wide as she put her feet on his shoulders. 'I had to ignore the inquisitive glances when I bought this at the shop in Highdale. I wanted something to celebrate the fact that we're back together again after a very long week.'

He leaned across and put a sudsy finger over her lips. 'One of the longest weeks of my life.'

He followed this with a kiss on her lips.

'That's too much of a contortion,' he said, turning himself round so that they were lying spoonshaped along the length of the bath.

She moved her head so that their lips could join in a long, lingering kiss.

'That's better,' Jason whispered, his fingers moving lightly over her body until his caresses began to drive her wild with frustration.

Extricating himself carefully, he stepped out of the bath, leaning back to bring her with him.

She laughed as he held her in his arms, gently patting her dry with one of the clean fluffy towels she'd prepared. Nicky was warm and relaxed as he carried her through into her bedroom. She shivered with anticipation as he laid her onto the clean, scented sheets.

It was blatantly obvious that she'd planned a seduction. But she knew this was an experience they both wanted. They desperately needed to reaffirm the fact that they were lovers, that they trusted each other and that maybe the future held something for the two of them...

Nicky lay back against the pillows. Jason's head was almost touching hers, but she could hear his steady breathing and didn't want to waken him. Outside, the moon seemed to be winking at her as it shone into the bedroom.

Nicky looked up at the ceiling. A cobweb was swinging from the light shade. This weekend she would find the time to blitz the place...unless Jason had any better ideas. She smiled to herself as she thought that domestic chores had no importance in her life. Mundane everyday problems had ceased to exist now that she and Jason were back together again.

A cloud moved across the moon and she sky became completely black. She wondered why it was that every time she tried to convince herself that she had a future with Jason, a tiny little doubt would creep back to niggle at her. This was something she would have to learn to live with if she wanted to hold onto her precious relationship with him.

He was stirring in his sleep. She snuggled against him and he opened his eyes, looking at her with such tenderness that she felt as if her heart would burst with happiness. The niggling doubts vanished, as they always did when he pulled her into his arms, and with a mutual desire they began to make love again.

Nicky was thinking how much easier it was to cope with her apprehension about Jason's reaction to her pact with Sue as she stood on the top of the hill above Fellside, looking down over the other side into what she'd started to consider her own secret valley. Since their idyllic night together a couple of weeks ago, they'd maintained the most wonderful rapport between them. Yes, it was true, people were beginning to notice—her colleagues, some of the patients—but she found she quite enjoyed being paired with Jason.

Furthermore, she also enjoyed the newfound bond she felt with the other two couples in the practice. Jane and Richard and Patricia and Adam hadn't actually asked her outright if there was a romance in the offing, but there had been pointed remarks and a few jokes about the time she and Jason spent together.

It was true they spent every evening and weekend when they were both off duty together. She'd almost forgotten that Sue hadn't yet put the record straight. It would happen some time, but meanwhile she was so happy that it didn't seem important any more.

Nicky looked down into her secret valley, moving slowly down the steep path so that she could catch a glimpse of the cottage she couldn't afford, her dream home that was way beyond her means. She'd been to see Jane that afternoon and this trek up to the secret valley was an impulsive adventure.

That first time she and Jason had walked up here she'd been surprised to come across this completely hidden dale as they'd walked over the top of the hill. She'd been even more surprised to see the cottage. She stopped her descent as she saw a man in overalls coming out onto the porch, then another man in jeans and T-shirt, his broad, muscular, tattooed arms seemingly innured to the cold temperature. She held back, not wanting to appear as if she were spying.

But the man with the tattooed arms looked up and saw her. He waved his hand. 'Are you lost, miss?'

'No, I just came to see if the cottage had been sold,' she called quickly. 'It looks a bit different to the last time I saw it.'

'We're doing our best to get it ready for the new owner who wants to move in at Christmas. It needs a lot of work but we're getting on top of it now.'

'You're doing a great job.' Nicky admired the new roof, the impeccable windows with their freshly painted frames and the high stone walls that defined the garden and kept out the sheep. She could hear hammering coming from the back of the house. It seemed as if a whole army of workmen was being employed to prepare the house for the lucky new owner.

'Come and have a closer look if you want, miss. You won't disturb us,' the man in the overalls called in a friendly voice. 'Me and Brian are just having a tea break before we do a bit more.'

The workman unscrewed his Thermos flask. 'You can have a drop of my tea if you like to keep out the cold.'

She smiled. 'I'd better be getting back. It'll be dark soon. But thanks anyway.'

She turned sadly and retraced her steps to the brow of the hill. It would only have made things worse if she'd actually seen the inside of the house because, from the smoke spiralling upwards, it looked as if they'd sorted out the fireplace and swept the chimney. As she started to walk down the other side towards Fellside she told herself there would be other cottages coming on the market. Little houses that she could afford. But would she fall in love with them as she had, inexplicably, done with this one?

Perhaps falling in love was too strong a description for the feelings she felt. She'd fallen in love with Jason, that was sure, but the house was an inanimate object and she mustn't invest it with some unknown power. It was merely made of stones and a roof, but it had really got under her skin.

Nicky glanced at her watch as she hurried down the

Fellside path towards the darkening valley. There wouldn't be time to call home before she did evening surgery. She glanced down at her muddy boots. The mud hadn't crept up the legs of the trouser suit hidden beneath her anorak. If she changed into her driving shoes and gave them a quick wipe over with a duster she would look reasonably smart. Anyway, the patients wouldn't be there to appraise her appearance. So long as she gave them her full attention that was all that mattered.

Jason was just leaving his consulting room as she entered the front door of the practice.

'What do you think of the Christmas decorations?'

She smiled as she glanced around at the tinsel and coloured paper trimmings that were strewn across the ceiling of the waiting room.

'Did you do all this?'

He laughed. 'No, it was Lucy. She said they always start on the decorations three weeks before Christmas. Apparently, the Christmas tree will be delivered tomorrow.'

He hesitated. 'I wondered when you were going to put in an appearance. I finished my afternoon clinic some time ago but I've been waiting around for you. And I thought if you'd decided to take the evening off I could stand in for you. I phoned Jane and she said you'd left Fellside ages ago.'

'I decided to go for a walk.'

'Up to your secret valley?'

'How did you guess?'

'You've talked about it often enough.'

Nicky sighed. 'Well, I won't be talking about it again. It's been sold. It's crawling with workmen pulling the place into shape. I couldn't have competed with that. Even if I could have afforded the price—which I couldn't—I couldn't have paid for the repairs.'

'That's what I thought,' he said quietly. 'So you'd best forget about it.'

'I already have,' she said breezily. 'I'm not going to get all worked up about a mere house. I've got my name down with the same estate agent and he's going to let me know when something comes up in my price bracket. Trouble is, there's a big discrepancy between my idea of the house I want to live in and how much I can afford.'

The phone in her consulting room was ringing. She gave Jason a wry grin. 'That's probably the estate agent phoning now to tell me about an absolute bargain of a place.'

'I'll hold on because I need to talk to you.' He hovered in the doorway as she hurried over to the desk.

'Sue!'

Nicky practically screamed her ex-flatmate's name down the phone as she recognised her voice immediately. Jason, looking startled, followed her into the room and closed the door.

He moved towards the desk. Sue's unmistakable voice could be heard clearly on the line. Jason, she noticed, had settled into a chair beside her.

'I'm just outside London. In the awful rambling suburbs I vowed I'd never live in, but beggars can't be choosers,' Sue said. 'I'm renting a flat in a not very salubrious area and I'm feeling all alone and dead miserable.'

'Give me the address,' Nicky said tersely. 'And your phone number.'

She reached for her pen.

'Will you and Jason come down and see me, Nicky...tomorrow, please? You don't work on Saturdays, do you? I'm feeling all mixed up.'

Nicky drew in her breath. She mustn't antagonise Sue

before she got to the truth. 'I've got this weekend off, but I'll have to check with Jason if—'

'I need to see Jason. Please, persuade him, Nicky!' Sue's voice rose to a crescendo that was clearly audible in the room.

Jason was nodding his head, a concerned expression on his face.

'Yes, we'll come down, Sue. We've got a lot to talk about, haven't we? I think we need to clear the air. A complete explanation would be a good idea.'

There was a long pause before Sue spoke again in a flat voice. 'I suppose if you and Jason are working together you'll have been discussing me.'

'Not exactly,' Nicky said carefully, glancing across at Jason. 'I was hoping you would agree to—'

'Look, I've got to go!' Sue lowered her voice. 'You promised to keep quiet. I couldn't bear it if you told him without me being there to explain. We can talk when you come down here. You will come, won't you? My life's a complete mess. Mike's dumped me for good. I've got nothing to live for. Everybody would be better off without me…'

The line went dead. Nicky immediately redialled but all she got was a bland recorded message. 'The number you have called…'

'I don't think Sue's in a very stable frame of mind,' Nicky said evenly. 'We ought to drive down to London as soon as I've finished surgery. I would never forgive myself if she did something drastic.'

Jason looked alarmed. 'She sounded hysterical from what I could hear. What's the explanation you were talking about?'

'I don't want to discuss it till I've seen Sue. And the sooner we get down there the better, because I'm afraid we might be too late. I'll never forget how I had to pull her through the bad times. I had to stay up all one night talking her out of committing suicide and the signs of this happening again are already there. As a doctor—'

She broke off as she heard the low drone of the patients' voices outside in the waiting room. It was obvious they couldn't go down to London until after the evening surgery, but as soon as she'd finished her professional commitments she would be on the road.

'Sue is doing her drama-queen act and thoroughly enjoying all the attention she's grabbing,' Jason said quietly. 'But you're probably right about her state of mind. It would be unwise to leave her alone all night in the state she's wound herself up into. We'll share the patients between us this evening and then go down to London together. My car will be quicker than yours.'

'Weren't you due to take the Saturday morning emergency clinic?'

'I'll phone Richard and see if he or Adam can take it.'

She nodded. 'I wouldn't be able to sleep tonight for thinking about Sue, so we'd better go.'

If Sue was simply putting on an act it wouldn't be a wasted journey, because at long last she and Nicky would be able to tell Jason the truth.

CHAPTER EIGHT

As NICKY pressed the bell beside Sue's name at the entrance to the block of flats she thought what a depressing place this would be to live in. It was worse than the dumps where she'd lived nearer the centre of London. Jason's car was now causing a lot of attention at the kerbside from a gang of kids who looked too young to be roaming the streets at this time of night. Jason went down the steps to speak to them and Nicky held her breath.

Nearing midnight in a dimly lit street on the outskirts of London wasn't the time or place for a confrontation. It didn't make any difference how young they were. If one of them had a knife...

She breathed a sigh of relief as a couple of uniformed policemen appeared round the corner and the youths scattered.

Jason came back up the steps after speaking to the police officers.

'They've promised to keep an eye on the car. I said we shouldn't be long. They told me we'll have to move before eight tomorrow morning when the parking restrictions apply, but I said we intended to be back on the motorway heading north again by then.'

Nicky pressed the bell yet again. 'I hope nothing's happened to Sue.'

'She's probably asleep by now. Perhaps we should—'

A tired-looking young woman came up the steps from the street and began inserting her key into the communal lock.

Jason gave her a winning smile. 'Excuse me, I wonder if you would mind letting us in. Our friend is—'

'Help yourself, dear,' the woman said in a weary voice. 'I couldn't care less. I'm not the landlady. I only have to live here, worse luck!'

They were inside within seconds, standing in the grubby, paint-peeling hallway, looking up at the bare boards of a long flight of stairs. Sue's flat was number fifteen. Nicky followed Jason up the stairs and along the landing at the top with its succession of identical doors until they stood in front of a partially painted brown door with the number fifteen chalked on the wall outside.

Jason knocked, quietly at first then much louder. The neighbouring door flew open and an irate man poked his head outside.

'Pack it in, mate! Some of us are trying to sleep. It's a bit late to come calling on Sue. She'll either be out on the town or fast asleep by now and—'

'We need to speak to her tonight,' Nicky said firmly. 'Have you seen her this evening?'

The man moved out into the corridor. He was only wearing a tatty pair of jeans. He scratched his bare chest as he pondered the question.

'Well, she was here around teatime 'cos she came to borrow some milk. Hasn't got much idea of how to look after herself, hasn't Sue. But I don't know what she was planning to do tonight. Look, why don't you come back tomorrow when—'

'Have you by any chance got a key for Sue's flat?' Jason interrupted.

The man pulled a face. 'You must be joking! People round here don't like—here, steady on!'

Jason had put his shoulder to the door and pushed hard. The wooden panels resisted, but creaked. He tried again, this time with all his force, and the door caved in. They hurried inside. Nicky tried to close the splintered door but it was impossible. The bare-chested man stood in the doorway, eyeing them with suspicion.

'I don't know what you're up to but—'

'We're both doctors,' Jason said tersely. 'Coming to check on our friend's health.'

'So you say. Seems a bit fishy to me. If you're not out of here in two minutes I'm calling the police.'

Nicky was trying her best to ignore Sue's neighbour as she looked around the chaotic room. Empty plates and mugs littered the small wooden table. Newspapers were strewn around the floor. The narrow bed in the corner was covered with a crumpled duvet but there was no sign of Sue.

Nicky called her name. There was a door leading off the main room. Jason had already gone through.

She heard him gasp 'Sue?' almost in disbelief.

Nicky hurried through to a tiny space which had obviously been little more than a store cupboard. Someone had rigged up a pipe with a shower head on the end and attached it to the wall above a crude plastic shower tray. Sue was crouched in the shower tray, her hands across her naked body, her eyes closed. Blood flowed from both wrists into the shower tray.

'Sue, can you hear me?'

Sue gave a low moan and opened her eyes. 'Jason! You came!'

Jason turned to ask Nicky to get the sheet from the bed so they could bind the wounds.

'Keep still while I examine your wrists, Sue. When did you do this—when?' Jason asked, as he took the first strip Nicky had torn from the sheet and began binding Sue's right wrist.

'Not long ago,' Sue murmured. 'I didn't want to live any more. I couldn't cope with—'

'Hush,' Nicky said, gently, as she tore up more bandages. 'Save your strength, Sue.'

Jason had improvised a tourniquet on both arms now so that the blood was no longer spurting out but seeping into the bandages at a slower rate.

Nicky had already phoned for an ambulance, stressing that she was a doctor with a patient who needed to be taken to hospital immediately. She wrapped towels around Sue as Jason lifted her from the shower tray and carried her over to the bed. There was an old towelling dressing-gown on the floor. Nicky remembered it as being a favourite of Sue's. When she'd been recovering from her termination of pregnancy operation she'd worn nothing else for weeks.

Carefully, she wrapped it around Sue's shoulders. Her intense pallor was alarming but only to be expected as she'd lost so much blood. Nicky checked on Sue's pulse again—it was fainter than last time.

'I'll go down and open the door for the ambulance staff,' she said tersely, hurrying away.

The neighbour in the doorway moved to one side. 'Sorry, dear. I reckon you really are a doctor, aren't you? I wouldn't have…'

She could hear the distinctive sound of the ambulance arriving as she raced down the stairs and flung open the door. She gave brief instructions to the paramedics carrying a stretcher.

Minutes later, Sue was safely inside the ambulance. Jason immediately fixed a glucose and saline drip to help counteract the dehydration.

'We'll determine her blood group as soon as we arrive at A and E,' he said, quietly. 'She's going to need a transfusion of blood because she's lost a lot.'

'How long is it since the patient slashed her wrists, do you think, Doctor?' one of the paramedics asked.

Jason looked at Nicky as he thought through the evidence. She also had her own theory on that one but she waited to see what Jason would come up with.

'I have a feeling that Sue had only just slashed her wrists minutes before we found her,' he said slowly.

Sue opened her eyes. 'You're right,' she said faintly.

'Were you actually hoping we would arrive in time to save you?' Jason asked gently.

Sue closed her eyes again and didn't answer, but the telltale tears that escaped down her cheeks told them that Jason had surmised the truth.

'I suspected it was a cry for help,' Nicky told Jason, as they sat outside the hospital side ward where Sue was now sleeping.

A staff nurse came across from the nurses' station, carrying a small tray. 'I thought you might like some coffee.'

'Thank you.' Nicky smiled as she took the welcome mug from the tray.

'Night Sister has just phoned the ward to ask if you could stay on a bit longer. When Sue wakes up she might be restless and difficult to handle if she hasn't got a friend or relative nearby. You know what attempted suicide patients are like, don't you, Doctor?'

'Unfortunately, yes,' Nicky said evenly.

Jason took a sip of his coffee. 'We were just discussing the possibility that Sue might have delayed her attempt so that we would find her before it was too late. But, in any case, even if it was a cry for help, we shouldn't leave her. I've phoned her mother's sister who lives in London. Sue used to be very close to her aunt when she was younger. She's assured me she'll be here first thing in the morning.'

The staff nurse nodded. 'You'll be able to go when the aunt arrives. But meanwhile we've put a couple of armchairs in Sue's room. Do you think you'll be able to get some sleep while you wait for your friend to wake up?'

'I could sleep standing up,' Nicky assured her.

She snuggled down in the armchair close to Sue's bed, smiling across at Jason as he attempted to make himself comfortable in the armchair near the door.

'Sweet dreams,' she mouthed.

He smiled back and blew her a kiss.

It seemed only seconds later when Nicky was awakened by someone touching her arm. She opened her eyes. In the dim light of the room she could see that Sue was reaching out towards her with the hand that wasn't encased in a splint. Nicky was instantly awake. Sue was whispering something.

Nicky stood up and leaned across towards her.

Sue frowned. 'Shh! Don't wake Jason.'

Nicky glanced across at him to assure herself that he was sound asleep.

'I'm not going to tell Jason,' Sue whispered urgently. 'It would ruin everything. Jason and I were meant for each other. It's always been like that. I know you're trying to take him from me but—'

'Sue, you've got everything wrong. Jason is very fond of you but—'

'Jason loves me. So don't you dare spoil it by telling him anything about how I said he'd made me pregnant. If you do I really will kill myself. It won't be a cry for help next time, and you would be responsible. Could you live with that for the rest of your life, Nicky?'

A cold hand clutched at Nicky's heart. With an effort, she was tried to remain dispassionate and professional. Sue was obviously very sick and Nicky couldn't take any chances.

'You need to rest, Sue. You've been through a bad time and you don't know what you're saying so—'

'Is everything OK?' Jason was stirring in his chair, rubbing his eyes as he looked across the room towards the bed.

'Sue is a little bit restless,' Nicky said quickly.

Jason stood up and came across to take hold of Sue's hand. Nicky noticed Sue's loving expression as she raised her eyes to look at Jason.

'Don't leave me, Jason,' Sue said, clinging to his hand. 'Change places with Nicky so that you can be by my side.'

Jason flashed Nicky a look which showed that he felt he had no choice but to indulge his demanding little surrogate sister.

'OK, if it will help you to sleep,' he said in a resigned tone as he settled himself down beside the bed. 'But you've got to close your eyes and try to sleep or I'll go away. Now, be a good girl because Nicky and I need our sleep even if you don't.'

Sue complied but remained holding onto his hand as if her life depended on it.

It was still in the predawn darkness when Nicky finally stirred herself in the armchair by the door. It had been a long time before she'd been able to sleep after her unpleasant encounter with Sue, but eventually she'd been able to drift off.

The noise of the ward awakening reminded her of her days as a junior hospital doctor. During the night she'd awakened to find Jason checking on the flow of the intravenous blood. Staff Nurse had also frequently checked on Sue, recording the state of her pulse and blood pressure.

Jason and herself had both agreed after Sue had been admitted to hospital the previous night that it was obvious their friend needed urgent medical help from a good psychiatrist. Jason had already set the wheels in motion. And it was Jason who'd insisted on phoning the sister of Sue's mother to alert her to the fact that her niece was in hospital and in need of some help and support from the family.

Nicky stretched in the chair, looking across to the bedside chair where Jason was still asleep. As if sensing her watching him, he opened his eyes. She walked across to check on Sue.

'How's the patient?' he murmured groggily.

'A better colour and her blood pressure's improved,' Nicky said.

Sue stirred at the sound of their voices. 'I feel awful but not as bad as I did last night.'

Nicky leaned across. 'It's going to take time but you've survived.'

'I didn't want to last night. I've got no money left. I gave it all to Mike when we were in Thailand. I was besotted with him and I thought I could keep him if I kept on giving him money. As soon as I was broke he dumped me.'

Sue began to sob. Jason put an arm around the heaving shoulders.

'Don't talk if it makes you feel tired, Sue,' he told her gently. 'Just rest...'

The girl shook her head. 'No, I want to tell you everything because you've been so good to me.'

Nicky held her breath. Had Sue had a change of heart?

Sue took a deep breath and the sobbing subsided. 'Oh, Jason, I should never have gone out with Mike. I met him at a wild theatrical party and I thought I'd fallen in love.

I'd no idea what he was really like. He's a bit of a bad type…been in prison a few times…'

Sue lay back against the pillows, staring up at the ceiling. 'Mum would have a fit if she knew what Mike was really like. I've a good idea he spent all my money on drugs. Anyway, I'm broke again, and I haven't got a job…and that flat is so depressing… Everything was just too much for me to cope with by myself…'

The sobbing grew louder and Jason made soothing noises. Watching Sue, Nicky could tell that she was getting the attention she'd desired. She longed to prompt her friend into making further revelations but she realised that it would be futile. Sue was in no fit state to reveal the truth to Jason even if she wanted to.

Nicky became aware that a tall, middle-aged lady had appeared at the door of Sue's room. She had a kindly face, surrounded by neatly cut grey hair. Jason hurried out through the door and began to talk to her outside in the corridor, obviously filling her in on some of the details. This must be the aunt.

Nicky leaned towards her distraught friend. 'Sue, I think you should rest now because—'

'No, let me tell you some more.'

Sue tried to reach her hand across but winced as she realised her arm was attached to a splint.

'I want to get it off my chest.' Sue lowered her voice, glancing towards the door to make sure Jason was still outside. 'I've always adored Jason, first in a brotherly way and later I tried to make him notice me as a woman, but he never took me seriously. But one day he will. You're trying to take him off me, but it's not going to work, Nicky. Can't you tell how he's falling in love with me? Did you see the way he put his arm round me just now?'

Nicky felt emotionally drained as she saw the agitated

expression in Sue's eyes. It was no good trying to reason with her, but there was one question she felt she must ask.

'I know you've suffered, Sue, but did you really intend to kill yourself last night?'

Sue took a deep breath. 'I didn't much care what happened but I needed somebody to be sympathetic to me. I told you I had an acting job to come to, didn't I? Well, that was wishful thinking because there's no job. I knew Jason would come last night if I sobbed a bit...'

She looked like a naughty little child as she peeped across the sheet that had been drawn up to her chin.

'I actually watched from the window until I saw you and Jason arriving. And then I sat in the shower tray with that razor blade and I gritted my teeth and—' She broke off in confusion as the tall, mature lady reached her bedside.

'How are you feeling now, Sue?'

Sue looked startled. 'I'm much better, Aunt Valerie. How did you know...?'

'I phoned your aunt,' Jason said evenly. 'You need family around you at a time like this.'

'And I've phoned your mother, Sue,' Aunt Valerie said gently as she settled herself in the chair Nicky had vacated. 'She's coming over to London on the first available flight.'

Sue closed her eyes. 'I suppose she'll want to know what this is all about.'

Jason leaned over the bed. 'My advice is to tell your mother everything. You may be surprised by how sympathetic she can be. She never used to make judgements when I was in difficulty.'

He paused. 'I've been having a word with the medical staff here and I think you'll find that they'll recommend some psychotherapy for you. Don't fight against this, Sue, because I really think you need professional help.'

Sue nodded. 'I need something to help me get my life back together again. You're probably right.'

Nicky felt a lump in her throat as she watched Sue gazing adoringly up into Jason's eyes. She so obviously idolised him...rather like she herself did!

He was reaching across the bed again. 'We've got to go now, Sue,' he said. 'Take care of yourself. You're in good hands here.'

'You'll keep in touch with me, won't you, Jason? Will you give my your mobile number so I can phone you?'

Jason hesitated before scribbling his number on a piece of paper. Sue clutched the paper as if it were a lifeline.

'Goodbye, Sue,' he said, planting a brotherly kiss on her forehead. 'Take care of yourself and be a good girl.'

Nicky awoke with a start as Jason pulled the car to a halt in front of her house.

'Wake up, sleepyhead. You've been asleep most of the way.'

She rubbed her eyes as she remembered being vaguely aware of the purring of the engine on the motorway before she'd gone back into her deep sleep.

She looked across and smiled. 'Would you like breakfast? It's Saturday so we don't have to rush off to work.'

He shook his head. 'I'll get something back at the flat. I had been going to suggest we go somewhere this afternoon but if you're too tired...'

'No, I'm OK, so let's go. No need to change any plans. What did you have in mind?'

His expression was enigmatic. 'Ask no questions. Can you be ready about three?'

She was intrigued. 'I don't see why not. But you'll have to tell me—'

'Wear something warm.'

'I always do now that I'm living near the Arctic Circle.'

Nicky pushed open the passenger seat door. He leaned across and hauled her back into the car so that he could kiss her on the lips for what seemed like a deliciously long time.

She smiled as she pulled herself away.

'That will give the neighbours no doubt about my dishonourable intentions,' Jason whispered.

It was good to hear the boyish timbre in his voice again. She smiled up into his eyes. 'I can sense the twitching of the net curtains so let me go in while I still have the remnants of a reputation.'

'If you insist.'

She closed the door and went into the house, pausing to look round after she'd inserted the key. He lifted his hand momentarily from the wheel before he drove off down the street.

The house felt very quiet after the bustle of the London hospital. It was so good to be back amongst the hills again. She made herself a piece of toast and a mug of instant coffee and carried them up to her bathroom. Quickly stripping off, she ran a bath and lowered herself into it, balancing the plate on the side between her shampoo bottle and the new bath foam.

She sprinkled the foam liberally into the hot water. Every time she used this brand now she would have wonderful nostalgic memories of Jason. But even as the welcome thought arrived, she felt a pang of apprehension. She didn't know what Sue would do next. How long could this idyllic rapport continue to exist between Jason and herself?

If and when the truth was revealed about the way she'd planned to set him up, would he be horrified that she was capable of such duplicity? Would she be able to convince him that she wasn't the least bit like his mother? She remembered how he'd told her weeks ago that he would find it hard to trust any woman after the way he'd seen his father suffer. When he knew about her duplicity, how could she persuade him that their relationship would be different, that it could go on for ever?

Because she knew, without a shadow of a doubt, that was what she really wanted.

CHAPTER NINE

NICKY dressed in the thick corduroy trousers she'd bought on a recent whirlwind shopping trip to Leeds, putting a long-sleeved T-shirt next to her skin and covering this with two layers of sweaters.

Jason grinned as she staggered out to the car.

'I feel like the Abominable Snowman,' she said. 'But you did say to wrap up warm. I'm wearing boots and thick socks so—'

'How about thermal underwear?'

He closed the passenger door on her and went round the front of the car to climb in beside her.

'I haven't bought any of that yet, but I'm thinking about it.'

He grinned. 'Is that a threat?'

She smiled. 'I don't think it would pose a problem.'

He leaned across and kissed her. She felt the familiar desire rising once more inside her as she tried to quieten that niggling inner voice that kept telling her it was too good to last.

She leaned back against the seat as he started the engine. 'So where are we going, exactly?'

'Not very far. You haven't time to sleep like you did this morning.'

'I've no intention of sleeping. I'm going to watch every part of this mystery tour. I think you're up to something, Jason.'

He laughed. 'How did you guess?'

He was driving up the hill towards Fellside but he continued past the end of the road that led down to Jane's and Richard's house.

'How was Jane when you saw her yesterday?' Jason asked, changing gear as he negotiated a hairpin bend.

'Enormous! And getting very frustrated at not being able to do very much. She'd had a show of blood earlier in the day so she was confined to bed.'

Jason frowned. 'I don't like the sound of that. With placenta praevia and a show of blood she really should be in hospital.'

'Apparently, that's what your friend James Beecham told her but she begged him to let her stay at home until after Christmas. She told him she was surrounded by doctors and wouldn't come to any harm. He was going to go out to see her yesterday evening and make an assessment of her condition. If he decides she must be admitted to hospital then she'll have to go along with it. You can imagine how she was feeling.'

Jason nodded. 'Poor Jane! I know how much she wants to spend Christmas at home, but at the same time she won't put her own or the baby's life at risk.'

'Absolutely not. She knows the score.'

Nicky looked out of the side window at the tall stone walls beside the narrow road. They had gone over the brow of the hill and were driving down the other side. Suddenly Jason slowed the car and took a right turn up a very bumpy track.

'Where on earth are we going? This isn't the track that leads to the cottage...is it?'

She broke off as she saw the strange, enigmatic expression on Jason's face.

'The very same. It's the track that you said could be easily mended. What do you think now you're driving on it?'

'It's pretty awful, but why should I care? It doesn't concern me. The new owner, who seems to have loads of money, will have to...' She drew in her breath, her thoughts racing ahead. 'Jason, why are we driving up here to the cottage? You haven't...?'

He didn't reply. She couldn't wait. 'You have! You're the new owner...aren't you?'

His expression relaxed. 'You're right about me being the new owner but wrong about me having loads of money. I've had to use all of the considerable sum I got from the sale of my London flat to buy the cottage and put aside enough to pay for the repairs and alterations.'

'But why did you buy it if...?'

She didn't dare to anticipate his reasons but when he spoke she felt a warm glow flooding through her.

'I thought it was a mad idea when you first said you liked it. But then, as we sat in the porch, it sort of grew on me, and I thought if it was what you wanted then I ought to buy it.'

'But you're the one who has to live in it,' she said quietly.

'I'd rather hoped that, as you'd fallen in love with the place, you might like to move in with me.'

He'd spoken so quietly that she wondered if she'd heard him correctly. The car ground to a halt in a flurry of stones beside the broken rickety garden gate.

'I'm going to have that gateway widened and run a drive straight up to the front door,' he was saying, as if he hadn't just pronounced the most exciting proposal of her life.

'Jason, I honestly don't know what to say about—'

'Then don't say anything until you've decided. It's a big step, I know. But we both know how well we get on together. Whether anything would change if we were actually living together...and out here in the wilds...only time will tell...'

His voice was faltering. She knew he was thinking about his parents' disastrous liaison. She found herself wondering if Jason's mother and father had gone through the ecstasy that they had at the beginning of their relationship, only to have it deteriorate and die. He'd told her that his mother had never been in love with his father but she must have felt something for him at the beginning. And the agonies of unrequited love that his father had gone through didn't bear thinking about.

'I think it would be wonderful, living up here with you,' she said softly.

His eyes were shining with tenderness as he pulled her closer. 'Do you really? I know you're an independent type and when you first saw the cottage you probably wanted to have the place to yourself, but—'

'I didn't want the place to myself,' Nicky said quickly. 'I hadn't thought the plan through, but somewhere along the way it would have had to include you.'

He kissed her slowly on the lips.

'That was putting the seal of approval on the idea,' he said, his voice husky with emotion.

She looked up into his eyes and saw a far-away expression. He was still not sure it could last.

'Jason, I know you experienced some hard times because your mother cheated on—'

'Let's not talk about it. That's all in the past. Dad's at peace now and Mum eventually found what she was looking for and I think she was genuinely happy towards the end of her life.'

'I didn't know your mother had—'

'Didn't I tell you? The man who finally made her happy was French. He was a qualified pilot, much younger than she was. My father always referred to him as Mum's toy-boy... Anyway, she moved to France to live with him and after the divorce came through they were married. He ran a flying school and when he wasn't working he used to take Mum flying. She was learning to fly when—'

Nicky waited until Jason had regained his composure.

'He was giving Mum a flying lesson, apparently. The weather wasn't brilliant when they set out. Her husband was a skilled pilot but he couldn't cope with the tempestuous weather that blew up soon after they'd taken off. They were on their way back to the airfield when the plane just seemed to drop from the sky, according to one eye-witness.'

Nicky sat very still, looking out at the wind blowing the leafless trees in the garden, imagining what it must have been like for Jason to hear such chilling news.

'Was your father still alive when...?'

'No, he...he'd died the year before.'

'Thank you for telling me the full story. It helps to know all about...where you're coming from. I feel so sorry for you.'

'I'm over it now,' he said in a determined tone as he leapt out of the car.

But as he opened the passenger door she looked at the sad expression in his eyes and knew that the past would always be with him. Was she the one who could erase those awful memories? The revelation that initially she hadn't been honest with him could be an awful setback. She would cross that bridge when she came to it.

As she stepped out onto the rough stones of the track she told herself she would give it her best shot. Looking across at her beloved cottage, which was how she could now think of it, she knew it would be wonderful to live here with Jason. In fact, it would be a dream come true.

She ran up the newly paved path to the front porch.

'Hey, steady on. Let me find the key.'

He pretended he'd lost it and she waited impatiently for him to stop fooling around.

The porch had been completely transformed already. The fragile wooden bench where they'd sat on that first day had been replaced by a robust slab of stone.

'That huge piece of stone used to be part of an ancient bridge over one of the moorland streams,' Jason told her, inserting the key into the sturdy oak, brass studded door. 'I found it in the stonemason's yard down at Highdale when I went out to see him on a house call. I had to persuade the workmen that it would be ideal for the porch and they agreed to collect and fit it.'

Nicky could barely wait to see what other changes had been made inside the house. But as the door swung open he turned to her, reaching down and swinging her up into his arms.

'There should be some kind of ceremony when the lady of the house moves in,' he said, his eyes twinkling.

'Is that what I'm going to be?' she asked, quelling the excitement that was rising inside her.

'Can't think of any other name, can you?' he said lightly.

She could think of any number—'mistress' perhaps—but first, foremost and favourite would be 'wife'. She dismissed the idea even as it emerged from her subconscious. That was taking the dream too far. She was content to be with him here in their love nest. She wouldn't look any further than the next day.

He carried her through into the main living room and put her down on a sofa in front of the wide open fireplace.

'It looks as if the workmen have had a fire,' he said. 'The chimney was due to be swept last week so—'

'There was smoke coming from the chimney yesterday,'

she said, as she foraged around among the logs and general debris of the wide, dusty hearth. 'Yes, the workmen have left us some firelighters and kindling.'

Jason began stacking small logs in the fireplace, before striking a match. 'I declare this house open,' he said, as the flames began leaping up the chimney.

Nicky looked up at the ceiling where the oak beams had been cleaned of cobwebs. A central light bulb without a shade looked as if it would work when they were connected to the source of electricity in this area. Looking down again, she saw that the uneven flagstones were partially covered with newspapers. The ancient, saggy sofa was the only piece of furniture apart from a couple of plastic chairs. But in spite of all its shortcomings, she still loved the place.

'The workmen told me they'd brought in the sofa, which they found on a dump, and the plastic chairs so that they could have tea-breaks in comfort,' Jason said, smiling as he watched her appraising the room. 'This is the only room that's remotely habitable. The roof and the floors are now sound everywhere but the central heating engineer doesn't come in until next week. I haven't had time to start thinking about furniture yet. That's where I'll need your help.'

She was thrilled at the prospect ahead. To be able to furnish her own home from scratch was another dream come true! All her childhood years of living in other people's houses, her adult years of dingy bedsits and the rented flat with Sue that had turned out to be a terrible problem. Now at last she had her own home…well, at least a share in Jason's for as long as their relationship lasted. She would offer to pay her whack towards the furnishing and whatever else she could afford. She didn't want to be a kept woman.

She went slowly round the house, noticing all the possibilities that were now on offer, making mental notes of what would be needed, what she thought they could afford.

There was one large bedroom—obviously that would have to be the master bedroom. Delicious shivers ran down her spine as she thought about the huge bed that would be a must for this room. Maybe a four-poster? Yes, that would be in keeping with the age of the house.

And there were three smaller rooms upstairs. In an ideal situation those could be for the children. She checked her thoughts as she ran downstairs again. One step at a time!

Jason was carrying boxes in from the car. The fragrant scent from the pine logs assailed her nostrils. The living room was warm and cosy already. Outside, the late afternoon sky was almost dark but Jason had lit a succession of candles and placed them on boxes around the room.

'And last, but not least,' he said, finally closing the door to the porch, 'our Christmas tree!'

From behind his back he produced a small, perfectly formed fir tree in a plant pot. 'No house should be without a tree at Christmas.'

Nicky smiled as she watched him setting it up proudly in the corner of the room. She sank down on the sofa. One of the remaining springs twanged loudly and she laughed.

'We're like a couple of kids playing at house,' she said.

He moved across and joined her on the lumpy sofa. He held her hand as they watched the flames from the fire licking up the chimney.

'We're not playing,' he said quietly. 'This is the real thing.'

She swallowed hard. If only it were! If only she dared to believe that this could last for ever!

The kettle on the small camping stove that Jason had brought in one of the boxes emitted a piercing shriek.

Jason jumped to his feet. 'Tea's ready!'

There was no teapot so they dunked their teabags in the boiling water.

'We're so well organised that we could move in tomorrow if we wanted to,' Jason said jokingly, as he handed her a biscuit.

She nodded in agreement. 'This room's perfectly habitable. I particularly like the artistic effect of the newspaper flooring. With a couple of rugs scattered over it and a mattress...' She stopped, her face setting into a mischievous grin. It was the idea of a mattress that had really given her romantic ideas.

Jason laughed. 'I'm game if you are. I'll nip back to the flat and get a few things. I've got one of those air mattresses I used to use for unexpected guests...and we'll need bacon and eggs for breakfast...'

'Breakfast! I wasn't thinking that far ahead. I just imagined how romantic it would be to lie in front of the fire, bathed in flames and candlelight. Are you sure the roof won't blow off or...?'

'We're as safe as houses, pardon the pun!'

She laughed. 'It's awfully dark out there.'

He planted a kiss on the tip of her nose. 'Sure you won't be scared while I'm away? I'll be as quick as I can.'

She assured him she was a big brave girl, but as the noise of the car engine receded in the distance she wasn't so sure. She put another log on the fire before curling up on the sofa, watching the flames. There was a small pile of logs on a piece of newspaper by the fireside. That should keep the fire going throughout the night. It was going to get very cold.

But they would be warm under Jason's duvet. Why were they being so mad when they both had warm flats to go to? In her case it was because she couldn't wait to begin her new life with Jason. She hoped it was something similar with Jason otherwise she had no idea why he was going along with it.

When she heard his car returning up the track she ran to the door and flung it wide open. She called out that she would help with the unloading but he told her to stay inside in the warm. He carried in yet more boxes of provisions, the duvet from the bed and the air mattress, which caused much hilarity when he spent ages inflating it.

'I couldn't find the pump,' he said, making loud gasping noises between the bouts of inflation.

She laughed. 'You look as if you're in need of cardiac resuscitation.'

'I'm in need of something,' he said, with mock frailty. 'Would you like to uncork the bottle in that box over there? We shan't need an ice bucket if you keep it in the far corner of the room.'

She'd never uncorked a champagne bottle before but, with Jason's instructions, she found it easier than she'd thought it would be.

'Rather like delivering a baby,' she said, as the cork eased itself out. 'You mustn't use undue force, simply let it slide out when it's ready.'

'Talking of which, I mean babies, I made a quick phone call to James to ask him how Jane was. He's agreed to let her stay at home as there's been no more bleeding, but at the first sign of any more complications with the placenta he's going to insist she's taken into the antenatal section of Nightingale Ward, down at Moortown Hospital.'

'I hope she's OK over Christmas.'

'So do I because we're all invited for Christmas Eve supper.'

'No! But she's supposed to be resting. How do you know about the supper?'

'James told me that she'd begged him to let her go ahead if she promised to delegate everything to all her willing helpers. He says you and I are on her list but you'd better pretend you don't know when you get the invitation. James has been invited so Jane will be in good hands if there are any problems.'

He tossed the fully inflated mattress on the floor in front of the fire. 'Want to try it out for comfort?' he asked, as he spread a blanket and sheet over it.

'Not by myself,' she said. 'We ought to see if it will hold the weight of two people.'

'I'm not sure if it will,' he said, easing himself down beside her.

She came readily into his arms, revelling in the feel of his hard, familiarly reassuring body. This was going to be one of many nights of love-making that they would share in this house. And if it didn't last she would always have her memories, but if it did...

She awoke because Jason had shifted his weight from the air mattress and she'd found herself going up in the air. She smiled as she watched him crouched over the fire, coaxing the recalcitrant flames into life. Outside, a red glow behind the trees told her that the winter sun was reluctantly casting its light over the valley. There would be precious little warmth out there, but inside, insulated from the strong wind, cosseted by the glowing fire, it was very cosy.

Jason filled the kettle from the bottles of water he'd brought with him and set it on the camping stove.

'I'm starving,' he said, rushing back to curl up next to her under the duvet. 'Do you realise we forgot to have supper last night? I'm going to cook us the biggest breakfast of bacon, eggs, mushrooms...but first...'

'That wretched kettle!' Jason exclaimed, leaping off the mattress as the whistling device announcing boiling water became too persistent to ignore. 'That's one item that will be banished from the house when we get the electricity on. Now, where were we...?'

It was midmorning before they managed to break off long enough to have breakfast. They picnicked on the mattress in front of the fire, scooping up the bacon and eggs with improvised wooden spatulas made from splinters of logs.

'I would have remembered knives and forks if I hadn't been in such a hurry to get back to you,' Jason said, as he mopped his plate with a piece of dry bread.

'That was the best breakfast I've ever eaten,' she told him, and she meant it. Food tasted so much better in an unusual, exciting situation.

She lay back against the pillow. It had been the happiest night of her life. Was the rest of their time in this house going to match up to it? She didn't even mind if they settled into a lower emotional plane, where contentment and companionship figured largely in their lives. Just so long as they didn't split up.

'Now, what would you like to do for the rest of the day?' Jason asked softly as he gathered her into his arms again...

The shrilling of Jason's mobile brought Nicky back to reality again. She stretched languidly, snuggling deeper under the duvet. A delicious feeling of unreality hung over her as she watched Jason foraging around amidst the assorted debris at the side of their love nest. Life was just too wonderful! The last few hours had been out of this world. She felt as if she were a goddess elevated to where she would live happily ever after and—

'Yes, Sue?'

Jason's brusque acknowledgement of the caller brought her back to earth. She'd forgotten that Jason had given Sue his number. This was probably the first of many interruptions to come.

'Yes, Nicky's here with me. I don't know why you're taking that attitude, Sue. It's perfectly natural for Nicky and me to be together. In fact—'

He stopped speaking and pulled the mobile away from his ear as Sue gave a loud shriek.

Nicky held her breath as he resumed listening.

'I don't think there's anything you can say that would disturb me about Nicky so fire away,' he said calmly.

He turned to look at Nicky and his hand covered the mouthpiece. 'Sue wants to tell me something I need to know about you. I think they must have increased the dosage of her medication but I'll humour her... Yes, I'm still here, Sue.'

His bantering tone had become incredulous. 'What did you say?'

He was listening intently now. Nicky sat up, pulling the duvet up in front of her. This was it! This was the moment Sue had chosen to come clean. She should have been prepared for it but she wasn't. She felt nothing but a great sense of loss as she watched Jason becoming increasingly more agitated. Every few seconds he queried what Sue had said, sometimes asking her to repeat it.

Finally he said quietly, 'Goodbye, Sue.' And terminated the call.

For a few seconds he was silent before he turned towards her again. 'I've just heard the most incredible story from Sue. Tell me it's not true that you planned to set me up for a fall, that your initial friendship was based on the need to humiliate me.'

'Jason, I can explain.'

'I hope you can,' he said.

'Did Sue tell you about the lies she'd told me about you?'

'Yes,' he said, his voice weary. 'She told me Mike had made her pregnant and she'd made out that I was to blame, that I was the one who'd forced her into a termination. And you believed her and then, when we met up at Highdale, you planned to exact revenge on her behalf. So you led me on. This whole relationship was aimed at setting me up for a fall and—'

'Jason, that was only at the beginning, before Sue told me she'd lied about you, before I'd fallen in love with you and begun a real relationship, a relationship that means more to me than—'

'It's no good, Nicky. How do I know? How can I trust you after this? How can I remember that wonderful evening in my flat when you came out of the shower and we practically made love, knowing that it was all a sham. And what about all the other times we—?'

'Don't! Please, don't remind me. I should have told you the truth once I'd found out that Sue had lied about you, but I couldn't. Sue had sworn me to secrecy. I was afraid of losing you and then Sue told me she would kill herself if I breathed a word to you at the hospital. Sue is in love with you, Jason. You've got to face that fact. She may be unstable but her ultimate goal is to make you love her.'

'I know,' he said, his voice calmer. 'She just made that perfectly clear. To me she's simply a naughty little sister who's always caused me trouble, and I expect no less from her. But you...'

He grabbed the phone again as the shrilling sound broke into his agonised words.

'Sue, don't call me back again. I'm trying to have a conversation with Nicky and— No, you're quite wrong. I'll always be your friend, and I'll help you through your present illness, but you can never be anything more than my little sister, and a very troublesome one at that. Now, if you call me back today, I shall hang up. I'll call you tomorrow at the hospital and by that time I shall expect you to have put all this nonsense behind you.'

He switched off his mobile and looked across at Nicky, his eyes glazed. 'I don't think I can take any more shocks today,' he said in a flat voice. 'If you'd like to gather your things together, I'll run you home.'

CHAPTER TEN

As NICKY parked the car in the surgery car park, she looked up at the sky to see if there was any sign of the promised snow. On the one hand, it would be wonderful if Highdale got snow on Christmas Eve. It was the sort of picture-postcard setting that looked idyllic with snow. On the other hand, if they were called out to any emergencies, especially at the remote homes in the higher dales and on the moors, it would make life very difficult for all of them.

As she walked in through the front door of the practice she thought how fortunate she was to be part of such a good medical team. Everyone pulled their weight and they dovetailed their duties to fit in with each other. Because it was Christmas Eve, all the doctors were technically on call. She and Jason had been asked to take the morning surgery and deal with any house calls, by reason of the fact that they didn't have the family commitments that Richard, Adam and Patricia had.

Jane, of course, was still confined to the house, forbidden to make any sudden movements that might upset the delicate state of her placenta. When Nicky had called in briefly yesterday, Jane had been very cheerful but obviously nervous as, indeed, they all were. It was as if the entire medical staff of Highdale Practice was holding its breath until this precious baby was born.

How on earth Jane would manage to remain calm at her supper party this evening, Nicky had no idea! It was true there would be no shortage of doctors, including James Beecham, but this would mean that everybody was keeping their eye on Jane and she wouldn't be able to move without it being a cause for concern.

'Hi, Nicky!'

Nicky looked up to where the sound of the voice was coming from. Lucy was at the top of a ladder, putting the finishing touches to the tinsel border she'd spread around the walls.

The waiting room now had so many Christmas decorations that it was difficult to move around without walking into a streamer! The Christmas tree in the corner was covered in presents for the staff brought in by grateful patients. There was a smaller tree beside Lucy's desk which was hung with small gifts for the children who came into the surgery over the Christmas period.

'Hey, be careful up there, Lucy! We can do without orthopaedic emergencies among the staff on Christmas Eve. We don't want to put you in plaster for Jane and Richard's supper party.'

Lucy grinned but continued with her decoration. 'I'm safe as houses... Talking of which, how's that cottage of Jason's coming along? When's the house-warming?'

Nicky's cheeks flushed. In the three weeks since she and Jason had spent the night in the cottage it had been assumed by the rest of the staff that she was somehow involved in the project. But ever since Sue's disturbing phone calls on the morning after their idyllic night, Jason's and Nicky's relationship had cooled to the point of non-existence.

Jason had told her that he wanted to come to terms with Sue's revelations in his own way. He needed time to sort out his emotions and he felt he should be on his own for a while. He'd been studiously polite in the surgery and everyone had been so busy preparing for Christmas that Nicky assumed their cold war had gone unnoticed. She, too, had been polite and professional with Jason, outwardly calm and together, but inwardly miserable. With a sinking heart she had been forced to admit to herself that it seemed inevitable now that their split would be permanent.

She went over to take hold of the bottom of Lucy's ladder.

'There's a lot to be done to Jason's cottage,' she said. 'It won't be finished for months.'

'You two are made for each other,' Lucy said firmly. 'You know that, don't you? I was only saying to my husband last night, if ever there was a true love match it's those two young doctors. Believe me, I've seen it happen with Jane and Richard, and Adam and Patricia, and when it does it's lovely! So romantic! Take it from an old married lady, the romance might dwindle a bit over the years but there's nothing like going through life together.'

Nicky gripped the rungs harder. This was precisely the kind of remark she could do without!

'I'd better be getting on with my work, Lucy. Will you be long up there? I don't want to leave you.'

'Just coming! Oh, Jason's out on a house call,' Lucy said, moving slowly backwards down the ladder. 'Shouldn't be long. It's only down in the village and it didn't sound very serious.'

Nicky waited until Lucy was safely at floor level before closing her door. She'd put some mock snow on the inside of her window, in keeping with the festive season and to match all the others in the practice. By the look of the glowering sky it wouldn't be long before they had the real thing. They were on high ground and whereas the valleys might have rain, it would snow up here.

She'd overheard Jason telling Adam, during a coffee-break at the surgery, that he was spending every available moment of his off-duty time visiting furniture and antique shops. Apparently, several rooms in the cottage were now furnished or partially furnished and the central heating had been installed, whilst the main fireplace had been turned into the centre of the house. With a sinking feeling, she realised that the cottage was obviously going to be Jason's bachelor pad.

Her intercom buzzed and Lucy told her that her first patient had arrived. There was a steady stream of patients throughout the morning, no serious emergencies—mostly coughs, colds and one patient wanting her to prescribe a cure for a hangover.

'I suffer something terrible over Christmas, Doctor,' the old farmer told her. 'Always have and it's getting worse as I get older.'

Nicky gave him a sympathetic smile. 'As you get older you ought to drink less, Bob. Your body can't take it any more. Try drinking a glass of water between each alcoholic drink and cut down as much as you can.'

The elderly man looked dubious. 'I used to be able to take ten pints and still be able to milk a full herd of cattle at the crack of dawn the next day.'

'Well, if you'd like us to run a series of tests on your stomach to see if it's functioning properly I can arrange that. Perhaps you should have a gastroscopy. That would mean going to the hospital and a doctor would put something down into your tummy and have a look around.'

The patient shuddered. 'I don't think I'm that bad. I'll try and take your advice and not go so wild this Christmas, Doctor.'

'I think you'll find if you drink less you'll enjoy your Christmas a lot more,' Nicky said gently, trying not to sound as if she was preaching. She didn't want to make Bob resentful. These old farmers were a tough breed who didn't take kindly to being told what to do.

'Now, I see from your notes that you haven't had a flu jab this winter,' she said.

'I don't like injections.'

'It will only take a second and you won't feel a thing,' she said, reaching for one of her small sterile packets. 'It's not a good idea risking flu this winter, especially at your age.'

Nicky looked up to see if she'd convinced him. Her patient pulled a face but slowly removed his jacket and grudgingly rolled up his shirtsleeve.

'Now, you didn't feel that, did you, Bob?' she said a moment or two later as she discarded the used syringe.

'Have you finished? Well, I'll be blowed! You can book me in for next year...if I'm still here.'

'I hope you have a happy Christmas, Bob!' Nicky said, as the elderly man shuffled towards the door.

'You 'n all, Doctor.'

She'd reached the end of the list. Only one more patient and she was looking forward to seeing this particular baby. It was the baby born after Harry's lorry had crashed into their car.

'Come in, Megan,' she said, as the mother opened the door. 'I've been dying to see young Jason. Oh, isn't he gorgeous?'

She took the small baby from his mother's arms and cradled him against her. There was something so special about babies before they could walk and talk. They looked up at you with such carefree, trusting, loving expressions. Jason was no exception. His bright blue eyes were clear and confidently trusting, and his little rosebud mouth curled into a smile.

'That's a definite smile,' his proud mother said. 'It's not wind, is it? I think he likes you.'

'He's adorable. Any problems?'

'Well, he's had a bit of a snuffle for the last few days. The girls picked up colds at school and I think he got it from them. I wouldn't have bothered you only I'm going to have a house full over Christmas and if it gets worse we won't want a crying baby to keep us awake at night.'

Nicky smiled. 'Jason doesn't look as if he ever cries.'

'Oh, believe me, he's got a good pair of lungs when he starts!'

'I see what you mean,' Nicky said, as she laid her small patient on the examination couch and reached for her stethoscope. Baby Jason squirmed, squalled and wriggled throughout her examination, but she was able to reassure Megan that his chest was as clear as a bell.

'Jason's cold is confined to the head. I'll give you some drops like the ones I've just put in his nose to help clear it, but apart from that there's nothing seriously wrong with him. He should be better in a few days. If you're worried, bring him back.'

Going back to the desk, she asked if she could call in her colleague, the original Jason, to see his namesake.

Megan gave a big smile. 'Oh, I'd love to see him. I was hoping he might be here.'

'He's been doing the house calls this morning but I think I heard him moving around next door…'

Jason said he'd love to see the baby he'd delivered in the back of the crashed car.

Young Jason stopped grizzling as the older Jason took him into his arms.

'He's a beautiful baby!' Jason looked across at Nicky. 'Makes it all worthwhile when you get a miracle like this, doesn't it?'

She nodded, her eyes misting. Seeing Jason holding his namesake had stirred up all the feelings she was trying to remain detached from. Marriage to Jason, babies coming in the future...that was an unattainable dream now.

Jason was handing the baby back to his mother. Nicky took a tissue from the box on the desk and blew her nose furiously.

'Thank you both ever so much for all you've done,' Megan was saying as she stood up and moved over to the door. 'Have a happy Christmas!'

'Happy Christmas!' they replied together.

Jason was following her patient out. Nicky felt a total sense of loss as she watched his retreating figure.

'Jason?'

He closed the door behind the patient and turned to look at Nicky. 'Yes?'

His eyes held that awful distant expression he'd worn for the last three weeks whenever he'd looked at her.

'Jason...I've missed you.'

He took a deep breath. 'I'm trying to sort out my feelings, Nicky. I need time. What we had was so precious, but now...'

'I never wanted to hurt you when I knew that Sue had lied about you.'

'But how could you believe I would be so awful to Sue in the first place?'

'I didn't know you then. I'd only met you once at Sue's dinner party. You were an unknown person and my first instinct was to take care of my vulnerable friend Sue.'

He ran a hand through his hair. 'Sometimes I think I understand your motives but whatever they were, you still deceived me at the beginning— No, don't say anything more, Nicky. I'll have to come to my own conclusions in my own time.'

He turned at the door and her heart leapt with hope.

'Are you going to Jane's party tonight?' he asked.

'Yes. I think everybody from the practice is going, aren't they?'

'I'll see you there.' His voice was cool and impersonal.

The door closed behind him and her sense of loss increased. At least she would see him tonight, but only as another guest.

'It's rather like a repeat of the supper party at our house on the evening of Emma's birthday,' Patricia said to Nicky as they all gathered in front of the fire in Jane's large sitting room.

Nicky smiled. 'The same cast, isn't it?'

'With two exceptions,' Jane put in from the sofa, where she was straining to hear the conversation having been forbidden to stand up. 'You all know James Beecham and his wife, Fay, do you?'

There was a general murmured agreement.

'So how's it all going, Jason?' asked James. 'It must be so peaceful up here among the hills. Nothing to do but treat the occasional cold…'

'Hey, steady on!' Jason said with a grin. 'It can be pretty hectic at times.'

'I expect it has its compensations,' James said, smiling as he looked knowingly at Nicky, leaving her in no doubt that he'd heard on the grapevine that she was having a relationship with Jason. It was going to come as a big shock to the local medical fraternity when they confirmed their split.

'Supper's ready, Jane,' Mrs Bairstow announced, wiping damp hands on her apron as she went over to the sofa. 'Now, you're not to move until that nice Mr Beecham says you can, and maybe Richard could—'

'It's all under control, Mrs Bairstow,' Richard said, as

he hurried across to take care of his wife. 'Don't worry, your little girl is in safe hands.'

Nicky remembered Jane telling her how Mrs Bairstow had looked after her since her mother died. She was obviously in a state of high nervous tension and with the supper to prepare it must have been very tiring for a woman of her age. But she looked like a strong country woman used to hard work.

'Is there anything I can do to help you?' she asked Mrs Bairstow as the flustered housekeeper hurried past her.

'Bless you, no, Doctor Nicky! I've got a couple of my nieces out there in the kitchen, putting the finishing touches before they help me with the serving, but thank you for asking. I can manage.'

Nicky smiled. 'I'm sure you can.'

Jason had put a hand under her arm, guiding her towards the door. The polite gesture meant more to her than it did to Jason, she reflected sadly. She enjoyed the fleeting contact with him. Glancing behind her, she saw that Richard had lifted Jane into his arms and was carrying her into the dining room, with James in attendance close behind.

When Jane had been propped up in a well-cushioned armchair at the head of the table, Mrs Bairstow and one of her nieces began serving home-made soup from huge steaming tureens.

Nicky looked round the table as the crackers were pulled and everybody extricated the little gifts from the insides and put on the funny paper hats. Last Christmas she hadn't known any of these friends and colleagues. What a difference a year made. She couldn't help wondering what next Christmas would bring.

'I had to operate on Belinda Turner, one of your patients, today,' James, sitting on her right, said quietly, so that only she could hear the information. 'I'll be sending you a written report but I was telling Jason earlier that it was a good thing you two brought her to my attention. As you know, she'd had three miscarriages, so I put in a Shirodkar suture as Jason suggested and it kept the foetus safe in the uterus. I'd hoped to take her to full term but today the uterus started to contract so I had to do a Caesarean.'

'How is Belinda?' Nicky asked anxiously.

'A bit weak, but holding her own. The baby, a tiny little girl, is eight weeks premature so we've got her in an incubator. Her lungs are immature but I'm confident she'll pull through. Belinda is absolutely delighted, of course. Insisting on being wheeled down to Intensive Care to see...'

James's voice trailed away. He was looking down the table at Jane who had suddenly doubled up in obvious pain.

'I thought this might happen,' Nicky heard him say under his breath as he sprang to his feet.

Richard was already holding his wife in his arms, carrying her towards the door, but not before the ominous red bloodstain on her dress had been seen by everybody.

There was a shocked silence as James rushed to the door, following Richard and Jane. James's wife, an experienced obstetric theatre sister, hurried after them. James turned at the door and beckoned to Jason.

'Will you help, Jason? I'm going to need an experienced obstetric team.'

Jason was on his feet already, making for the door.

After a brief silence, everyone started to talk in hushed tones. Minutes later, Richard appeared briefly in the open doorway.

'We're taking Jane to hospital. Do, please, stay on, won't you? Mrs Bairstow has cooked an enormous supper. I'll phone from the hospital.'

Nicky felt a lump rising in her throat. Richard, normally

so ebullient and lively, sounded utterly dispirited. The emergency that they'd all hoped wouldn't happen had been thrust upon them. It was nobody's fault. Even if Jane had remained on complete bed-rest, her misplaced placenta could have partially ruptured, as it obviously had.

But could they save the baby? It would be fighting for its life now as it struggled to survive with only a partial lifeline to its mother. Two precious lives were at risk.

CHAPTER ELEVEN

IT WAS a relief to escape from the party that had become more like a funeral. The dispirited guests had made valiant attempts to do justice to Mrs Bairstow's Normandy pheasant but appetites had diminished with the strain of the emergency. As they'd sat around in the sitting room, sipping coffee after the meal, everyone had been quiet and subdued, waiting for that phone call from Richard.

Adam had phoned the hospital and asked to be kept in touch with proceedings. He'd been told that James was operating on Jane but they had no details yet. The party had broken up as the evening had worn on and there had still been no news.

Nicky drove back to her little house and let herself in. Making straight for the kitchen, she made a pot of strong coffee. She wanted to stay awake so that she could phone the hospital for a progress report from time to time. Taking the coffee through to the sitting room, she curled up on the sofa in front of the fireplace and switched on the radio. One of the cathedral choirs was singing Christmas carols. Her eyes moistened and then tears streamed down her cheeks.

She'd thought that this would be her happiest Christmas ever, but her precious relationship with Jason was now shattered and Jane was in a critical state in hospital.

She sipped her coffee as she tried to pull herself together. James was a brilliant obstetrician. If anyone could save Jane and the baby, it was James. But sometimes there were complications that couldn't be overcome. What if—?

Her mobile started ringing. She grabbed it.

'Hold the line, I have a call for you.' It was the cool, impersonal voice of the hospital switchboard operator. Nicky recognised the background noises. 'Go ahead, Dr Carmichael.'

She waited, her heart thumping an agonised tattoo. And then, seconds later, Jason came on the line.

'Nicky, They're both OK...but only just.' Jason sounded tired. 'It was touch and go for both of them for a while. Jane has lost a lot of blood and the baby wasn't breathing when James delivered. The baby's condition is now stable and Jane is exhausted but she's sleeping peacefully. We've only just got out of Theatre.'

'And the baby? What is it?'

'It's a girl.'

Nicky smiled. 'Ah! A little sister for Edward. They're going to call her Hannah.'

'How do you know?'

Nicky's smile broadened.

'We had to talk about something to get Jane through her boring afternoons, and Patricia and I used to discuss names with her. Jane chose the name Hannah if it was a girl. She deliberately hadn't watched any of her scans and she'd asked not to be told the sex of her baby. To be honest, I think she was having grave doubts that there would be a baby towards the end. She told me it was all so different to her first pregnancy when she produced Edward with no problems at all.'

'Nicky...?'

Her heart turned over as she heard his gentler tone. He hadn't said her name like that since—

'Nicky, I'd like to see you. Will you come out to the cottage with me?'

'When?'

'I'll pick you up in about half an hour.'

She swallowed hard. 'I'll be ready.'

Either this was going to be Jason's way of completely ending their relationship or... Her heart was churning with emotion. She was on a roller coaster, unable to stop the journey towards her destiny. She wouldn't pack anything. If she put even so much as a toothbrush inside her shoulder bag, it would be tempting fate.

Nicky changed into corduroy trousers, two sweaters and an anorak, opened the curtains and stood watching the deserted street from the window. Earlier on, Christmas revellers from the pub and the midnight service at the church had been singing carols in the street, but now everything was quiet.

She hurried to the door as she saw Jason's car gliding towards her house. He leaned across and opened the passenger door.

'Such a relief that Jane's OK,' she said, climbing in. The strained atmosphere between them was palpable.

'There's a great celebration going on at the hospital, but I wanted to stay at the cottage,' he said quietly, his eyes on the road as he drove out of Highdale.

Nicky remained silent, longing to know if this was going to be the beginning or the end of their relationship. She was relieved when Jason drove up the newly gravelled drive in front of the cottage. The security lights flooded the garden as they approached, lighting up the tall trees that looked like ghostly statues. It all seemed so peaceful.

Jason put his key in the sturdy oak door, holding it open for her. She went inside, feeling amazement at the transformation that had taken place.

He disappeared into the kitchen. While she waited for him to return she looked around the living room. She could hardly believe that this was the dingy room they'd slept in only weeks before. The dimmed wall lamps illuminated the new white paint between the oak beams, casting cosy shadows over the comfy, squashy sofas and chairs.

Jason returned with a bottle of champagne and poured out a couple of glasses. The central heating had warmed the room but he knelt by the hearth, putting a match to the firelighter and logs that were already set in the antique iron grate. She found she was holding her breath until he turned round to look at her. As he smiled, that heartrending smile she knew so well, she relaxed. Maybe it was going to be OK, maybe this was a new beginning...

'To Jane and baby Hannah!' he said, clinking his glass against hers.

He sat down in the fireside chair at the other side of the fireplace. Nicky watched him from the sofa, taking another sip to steady her nerves. She couldn't wait any longer.

'Jason, this isn't just a celebration for Jane, is it?' she asked.

He looked across at her steadily. 'The birth of Jane's baby acted as a catalyst for me. As that dear little girl gave her first cry I wanted to cry with her. I wanted to cry for the precious moments I've wasted over the last three weeks.'

She froze, her pulses racing as his eyes met hers, but she didn't speak. The moment was too poignant.

'When I heard you'd deceived me, all the pain I'd felt in the past overwhelmed me. I couldn't sort out my feelings. I wanted to go on loving you but I felt unable to trust you. But tonight I realised that what we have is so precious it can't be broken because of some silly pact that was dreamed up.'

She put down her glass. 'Jason, I didn't know that Sue had lied about you. I acted on impulse because I was simply trying to do something to ease Sue's suffering. I just wish I'd been able to come clean earlier. She actually phoned me this week to say she was sorry for all the trouble she's caused me. She begged me to forgive her so that we could be friends again.'

'And have you forgiven her?'

Nicky pulled a wry face. 'I had to. Sue is the sort of person who will go around wreaking havoc with other people's lives and expect everyone to forgive and forget.'

He smiled knowingly. 'That sums Sue up exactly. She phoned me only yesterday to say that she thought the psychotherapy was helping her to get sorted out because she now realised how silly it would be to try and change our brother-and-sister relationship. She's sorry for everything she did to try and break us up.'

Jason got slowly to his feet, crossing over to the sofa. 'And I'm sorry I doubted you, Nicky. The last three weeks have been hell!'

He pulled her against him. She looked up into his expressive eyes, revelling in the tenderness she saw there, a tenderness that mirrored her own feelings.

'It's been hell for me, too,' she whispered.

Slowly, he bent his head towards her. She savoured the moment when his lips claimed hers. Being in Jason's arms was like coming home.

'Nicky, will you marry me?' he said, his voice husky with emotion.

She held her breath. Was the dream coming true? Had Jason actually asked her to marry him?

She looked up into his eyes, moved almost to tears by the passion in his voice.

'Yes,' she whispered.

He folded her in his arms and kissed her tenderly and slowly on the lips. She melted against him, knowing that this was where she belonged...for ever.

'Would you like to check out the new four-poster bed?' he murmured.

Liquid desire was stirring deep down inside her. It had been so long since they'd been together.

She snuggled against him. 'Mmm...I'd love to.'

He scooped her into his arms and carried her upstairs.

The first thing Nicky she noticed when she awoke was the silence. There wasn't a sound coming from outside in the garden. Jason was still sleeping peacefully. She tiptoed to the window, pulling back the heavy curtains to reveal the Christmas morning scene she'd hoped to find.

In the night the garden had become enveloped in a thin blanket of snow. The branches of the trees dripped frosty icicles, and from the sky came the steady fall of snowflakes, landing silently on the white carpet below.

Jason was already raising his head from the pillow as the bright light of morning lit up the room.

'Happy Christmas, darling,' she said, hurrying back to the warmth of their bed. 'It's been snowing. I've never seen such a beautiful scene. It looks just like a Christmas card!'

He put an arm round her bare shoulders and pulled her against him. 'Would you believe me if I told you that I'd ordered the weather especially for our engagement party?'

She laughed. 'Who's coming to the party?'

'Just the two of us...when we get home from Patricia and Adam's Christmas lunch. Next year, after we're married, we could host the Christmas lunch here and invite everybody from Highdale Practice. What do you think?'

She giggled. 'I can't cook very well.'

He laughed. 'Neither can I, but we can learn a lot in a year. There's lots of things we need to learn about being married...but the good thing is you get a long time to perfect it. By the time we get to our golden wedding...that's fifty years isn't it? By the time we get there we'll know everything there is to know, everything about how to bring up children and grandchildren and—'

'Steady on, let's go one step at a time,' Nicky said, but it made her so happy to know that Jason was thinking that far ahead. She would never spoil his dream of the future. It was the same as hers.

'How about a wedding in the New Year?' he said, drawing her closer.

'Easter would be perfect! Spring flowers, lambs gamboling in the fields, much warmer weather than we're having at the moment and—'

'You're not cold, are you?'

'I shivered at the window but that was because I stayed too long looking at the snow.'

He began to caress her skin, his fingers lingering in ways he knew would drive her wild with anticipation. 'Yes, you do feel cold. Would you like me to make you warm again?'

She murmured something inaudible as she gave herself up to their heady love-making...

EPILOGUE

'The snow's definitely getting thicker,' Nicky said, looking out of the kitchen window as she scrubbed at the final saucepan. 'I hope everybody gets home before it starts drifting on the roads.'

Jason reached over and took the cleaned pan from her hands. 'Most of them haven't far to go—Greystones, Fellside, Highdale village. Sue and Clive might have trouble getting out of Highdale valley, but once they're on the main road they'll soon be at his parents' house in Leeds where it will probably all have melted.'

He put his arm round her waist, removing the tea towel she'd wrapped around herself as she'd tackled the washing-up that wouldn't go in the dishwasher. 'That's enough domestic chores for the day. Come and sit by the fire with me. Would you like a brandy to go with your coffee?'

'No, I think I'll pass on that,' she said, curling up on the sofa as she watched Jason pouring himself a glass.

He tossed another log on the fire and leaned back in the sofa, his arm around her shoulders.

'It was a good Christmas party, wasn't it?' Nicky said, gazing contentedly into the fire. 'I remember when you suggested it last Christmas I thought you were mad. Neither of us could cook and—'

'We can now! The kitchen is full of cookery books.'

She laughed. 'Yes, but when do we ever find time to read them? Mind you, I think our turkey was cooked to perfection.'

'Good thing I set the alarm and dragged myself out of

bed at the crack of dawn. That was an effort, I can tell you!'

'Yes, but you did come back again, didn't you?'

He gave her a rakish grin. 'Did I? Ah, yes, I think I remember something about Christmas wrapping getting mixed up with the sheets and duvet and then we had to spend ages sorting it out just so that you could take Patricia up to see the four-poster. Did she like it? Was it worth clearing up for?'

'She loved it. Everybody who's seen it loves it, including me!'

'And me!'

'Everybody thought we'd worked wonders on the house since our wedding. It was all still pretty basic at Easter when they came for the reception.'

Jason laughed. 'It was even more basic last Christmas. I'm glad we've called it Christmas Cottage. We'll have many memories of Christmases as the years roll by, but these first two have been extra special.'

Nicky smiled. 'What a difference a year makes! Even Sue seems to be getting her life sorted out. I'm glad we stayed in touch. I'm glad she went to live with her aunt for a while while she was having psychotherapy. She's still seeing a consultant on a regular basis but she certainly seems much stronger.'

Jason nodded. 'She met this new boyfriend at drama college when she was eighteen, didn't she? Apparently they went out a couple of times and then drifted apart. But it seems to be working this time.'

'I think he's good for her. And his family in Leeds sound like nice, friendly people. Sue likes them, anyway, which is the main thing.'

'They should have arrived back in Leeds by now, if they got through the snowy part of the dale.'

'Apparently, according to Jane and Patricia, it's unusual to have two white Christmases in succession, as we've had. I reckon it's because you've been wishing so hard for white Christmases that you've changed the weather pattern up here.'

She giggled. 'Nobody's complaining. I'd better start wishing now for next Christmas.'

A log fell onto the hearth. Jason leapt to his feet and put it back in the fire with the ancient iron tongs they'd found rusting away in a scrap yard. He stood for a moment, his back to the fire, looking down at her.

'What were you discussing with Patricia and Jane up there in the bedroom...apart from the four-poster, I mean? Anything I should know about?'

She hesitated, knowing that she couldn't hold her wonderful secret much longer.

'It was a bit of a coincidence really. Patricia's thinking of coming back to Highdale Practice full time again. Apparently, her sister, who used to look after Emma when Patricia first came here, is looking for a job and has offered herself as mother's help. That would suit both of them so Patricia was sounding out Jane about the possibilities. I actually said that I'd like to work part time in the spring.'

Nicky was watching his reaction as she prepared to surprise him with her wonderful news.

He looked puzzled. 'Well, if you'd like to spend more time at home then— Hey, you're not telling me that...?'

'I did a test this morning. I planned to tell you before everybody came and then Sue and Clive arrived even before I was out of the bathroom.'

He held her against him. 'The test... What...?'

'It was positive. I'm pregnant.'

He pulled her closer, rocking her backwards and forwards as if anticipating the movements they would make when they held their own precious baby.

'You've made me so happy, Nicky,' he whispered. 'I didn't know marriage could be like this.'

'Neither did I.' She touched his face, pulling his lips against hers.

'Did you tell Patricia and Jane the good news when you were discussing the staffing arrangements?'

'No, of course not! Not before I'd told you.'

Jason grinned. 'But I bet they had a good idea when you said you were thinking about working part time.'

She nodded. 'I think they did, but they were too discreet to say anything. I think I'll go and phone them now, put them out of their misery. After which I thought we could go and ruffle up the four-poster again. It won't harm the baby. Trust me, I'm a doctor.'

He stooped and kissed her on the lips. 'Why don't you delay those phone calls until tomorrow?'

She snuggled against him. 'I think I might just do that…'

Modern Romance™
...seduction and
passion guaranteed

Tender Romance™
...love affairs that
last a lifetime

Sensual Romance™
...sassy, sexy and
seductive

Blaze
...sultry days and
steamy nights

Medical Romance™
...medical drama on
the pulse

Historical Romance™
...rich, vivid and
passionate

29 new titles every month.

*With all kinds of Romance for
every kind of mood...*

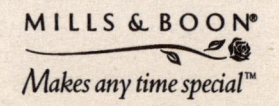

MILLS & BOON®
Makes any time special™

MAT4

MILLS & BOON®

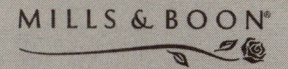

Medical Romance™

DOCTOR IN DANGER by Alison Roberts

Five years ago, Max and Georgina split when he objected to her job as a helicopter rescue paramedic. He'd wanted a family, not daily drama. Now, realising his love for Georgina, Max takes a job as the helicopter base's doctor. Meanwhile, Georgina has reassessed her life and all she wants now is that family —with Max. But then Max's helicopter flight crashes…

THE NURSE'S CHALLENGE by Abigail Gordon

When locum Dr Reece Rowland arrived in Alexa's life, he awakened feelings in her that she had never felt before. Alexa was determined to get closer to this fascinating man, but Reece's complex and painful past had built strong emotional barriers. Winning his love was going to be the challenge of a lifetime!

MARRIAGE AND MATERNITY by Gill Sanderson

How was Sister Angel Thwaite to know that saving a newborn in her neo-natal unit would change her life? The orphaned baby's uncle, Mike Gilmour, was the hospital's new cardiac surgeon—and Angel's ex-husband! Brought together, Mike and Angel were reminded of the life they could have had—and still could if they dared to be husband and wife again.

On sale 4th January 2002

Available at most branches of WH Smith, Tesco, Martins, Borders, Eason, Sainsbury's and most good paperback bookshops.

MILLS & BOON

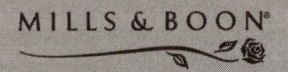

Medical Romance™

THE MIDWIFE BRIDE by Janet Ferguson

With a challenging new job and lovely new home, midwife Ella Fairfax isn't looking for love. At least not until she sets eyes on her handsome neighbour, Patrick Weston! Both single parents with medical careers, they're made for each other. But there is another woman in Patrick's life… is Ella wrong to dream of being his bride?

THE CHILDREN'S DOCTOR by Joanna Neil

Paediatrician Anna Somerville knew wealthy, successful heart surgeon Carlos Barrantes was out of her league, despite the sizzling attraction between them. Anyway, she would be leaving the island soon. But Carlos was overwhelmed by his feelings for Anna, and wanted to find a way to make her stay…

EMERGENCY: MOTHER WANTED by Sarah Morgan

Casualty officer Keely Thompson is determined to prove to dynamic A&E consultant Zach Jordan that she is no longer the scatty teenager who once declared her love for him. But Zach has also changed —he's now a single father! He and his daughter need Keely's help, but why can't Zach see her in the role of wife and mother?

On sale 4th January 2002

Available at most branches of WH Smith, Tesco, Martins, Borders, Eason, Sainsbury's and most good paperback bookshops.

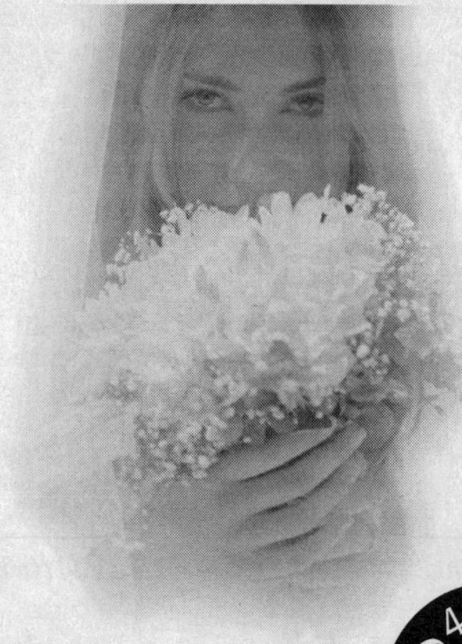

MILLS & BOON

FOREIGN AFFAIRS

*A captivating 12 book collection of sun-kissed seductions.
Enjoy romance around the world*

DON'T MISS BOOK 4

outback husbands–
The fiery heart of Australia

Available from 4th January

*Available at most branches of WH Smith,
Tesco, Martins, Borders, Eason, Sainsbury's
and most good paperback bookshops.*

FA/RTL/4

MILLS & BOON®

STEEP/RTL/9

The STEEPWOOD Scandal

REGENCY DRAMA, INTRIGUE, MISCHIEF...AND MARRIAGE

A new collection of 16 linked Regency Romances, set in the villages surrounding Steepwood Abbey.

Book 9
Counterfeit Earl
by Anne Herries

Available 4th January

Available at most branches of WH Smith, Tesco, Martins, Borders, Eason, Sainsbury's, Woolworths and most good paperback bookshops.

FREE

2 BOOKS
AND A SURPRISE GIFT!

We would like to take this opportunity to thank you for reading this Mills & Boon® book by offering you the chance to take TWO more specially selected titles from the Medical Romance™ series absolutely FREE! We're also making this offer to introduce you to the benefits of the Reader Service™—

- ★ FREE home delivery
- ★ FREE monthly Newsletter
- ★ FREE gifts and competitions
- ★ Exclusive Reader Service discount
- ★ Books available before they're in the shops

Accepting these FREE books and gift places you under no obligation to buy; you may cancel at any time, even after receiving your free shipment. Simply complete your details below and return the entire page to the address below. ***You don't even need a stamp!***

YES! Please send me 2 free Medical Romance books and a surprise gift. I understand that unless you hear from me, I will receive 4 superb new titles every month for just £2.49 each, postage and packing free. I am under no obligation to purchase any books and may cancel my subscription at any time. The free books and gift will be mine to keep in any case.

M1ZEC

Ms/Mrs/Miss/Mr ....Initials ....
BLOCK CAPITALS PLEASE

Surname ....

Address ....

....

....Postcode ....

Send this whole page to:
UK: FREEPOST CN81, Croydon, CR9 3WZ
EIRE: PO Box 4546, Kilcock, County Kildare (stamp required)

Offer valid in UK and Eire only and not available to current Reader Service subscribers to this series. We reserve the right to refuse an application and applicants must be aged 18 years or over. Only one application per household. Terms and prices subject to change without notice. Offer expires 30th June 2002. As a result of this application, you may receive offers from other carefully selected companies. If you would prefer not to share in this opportunity please write to The Data Manager at the address above.

Mills & Boon® is a registered trademark owned by Harlequin Mills & Boon Limited.
Medical Romance™ is being used as a trademark.